Paul Betts

THE MAN

IN THE CANAL

SEQUEL TO
PHU BAI & KAGNEW STATION

PAUL BETIT

Cover: The blue and yellow of the Scandinavian cross has been in use as Sweden's colors since King Magnus II adopted the hues for the royal family's coat of arms in 1275.

Library of Congress Catalog Card No.: 2013955825

Betit, Paul
Phu Bai: A Vietnam War Story/Paul Betit
p. 208
1. Fiction-Mystery & Detective 2. Fiction-Suspense
3. Fiction-War & Military
1. Title.

Softcover ISBN: 978-1-934949-85-6
Kindle ISBN: 978-1-934949-86-3
Smashwords ISBN: 978-1-934949-87-0

Published by

JWB

Just Write Books
Topsham, ME 04086
207-729-3600
www.jstwrite.com

Printed in the United States of America

To Laura,
who truly
brings joy
to our family

What reviewers are saying about Phu Bai

"This fast-paced murder mystery grabs readers early in the story. Filled with suspense throughout, this is a book you will likely to read nonstop."
—Lloyd Ferris, *Maine Sunday Telegram*

"…its rapid pacing makes for good beach reading."
—Kirkus Discoveries

"Betit writes vividly …His narrative is crisp, fast-paced and filled with action …"
—William D. Bushnell, *The Times Record*

"Many readers are bound to enjoy this book for its rap-id-fire plot and near-cinematic view of the Vietnam War."
—Lloyd Ferris, *Maine Sunday Telegram*

Author's Note

The Man In The Canal completes the trilogy about the exploits of U.S. Army CID investigator John Murphy I envisioned when I began writing the series in 1999.

This novel was the most challenging to write. The first two stories were set in South Vietnam and Ethiopia, two countries I had lived in for a considerable amount of time. *The Man In The Canal* is set in Sweden, a country I didn't step foot in until I had written forty percent of the narrative. I must have visited the Scandinavian country on the warmest, sunniest days of the year. I saw little of the fog and drizzle prevalent in most Swedish films I've watched.

As with most novels, *The Man In The Canal* is a collaboration. I had a lot of help.

I learned a lot about the challenges faced by the American military deserters in Sweden during the Vietnam War era by reading *American Deserters In Sweden,* a work of nonfiction written by Thomas Lee Hayes, an American clergyman who ministered to their needs for a time.

Reading the Martin Beck stories, crime novels written by the legendary husband and wife team of Sjowall and Wahloo, provided me with background into Swedish police methods in use in 1971, the time period during which *The Man In The Canal* takes place.

My conversations with Swedish hockey players Ulf Samuelson, Bjorn Melin, Dennis Persson, Jhonas Enroth, David Rundblad and Oliver Ekman-Larsson provided me with insights into Swedish culture, cuisine and language. They are all cool dudes.

I also appreciate the patience exhibited by the dozens of people I conversed with in Mariestad and its environs during my research trip to Sweden. Their cordiality and willingness to answer the dumbest of my questions was greatly appreciated.

During the editing process, Lisa Wesel, a former newspaper colleague, provided me with great feedback. She made sure I got details right and helped eliminate redundancies.

Faith Perry deserves special thanks for correcting my goofs, expelling redundancies and making the narrative leaner and meaner.

As usual, the best editor of my work is my wife, Debbie. Not only does she fix the typos and help clean up the grammar, but she also takes the time to read the manuscript aloud to me. That exercise is primarily responsible for the conversational tone of the series.

Paul Betit

THE MAN
IN THE CANAL

July 1971

LARS HAD WAITED all summer for Bjorn to come with his family from Stockholm and move into the little red cottage around the corner from his home.

On the first morning following Bjorn's arrival, the two boys got up early, before anyone else, and hurried down the well-worn path through the woods to the canal. A cacophony of sound greeted them as the birds nesting in the large grove of trees welcomed the morning sun with a variety of chirps, trills, cackles and whistles.

For a city boy like Bjorn, the early morning noise in such a serene setting was overwhelming. He was used to the sounds of Stockholm traffic, the blaring of horns and the singsong klaxon of police cars speeding to the scene of a crime or to an accident.

"Lars, I'm scared," he admitted.

"Don't worry," his young friend answered in a calm voice. "There's no one around. Nothing can hurt us."

Lars picked up the pace. "I want to get to the lock before old man Samuelson gets up."

Lars needed Bjorn's muscle to help him operate the long wooden lever that controlled the water in the lock. A scrawny 11-year-old, Lars was sure he still wasn't strong enough to handle the device by himself.

It took the boys about ten minutes to walk through the woods to the canal. When they emerged from the trees, they walked along the tow path beside the canal for another minute before reaching the wooden platform that housed the large metal gears which controlled the water level in the lock.

Bjorn helped Lars lift the large wooden stave off the ground,

1

where the old lock keeper had left it the night before, and slide it into the slot at the top of the gear assembly.

Before they tried to push the lever, Lars glanced down into the lock to check the water level. It was low. At the far end, he noticed an object floating up against the lock's wooden doors.

Lars pointed. "What's that?"

The two boys walked over and looked down.

"It looks like a big doll," Bjorn stated.

For a moment, Lars agreed. It did look like a giant-sized rag doll, with its large vacant eyes staring into space, ivory-colored skin drained of its natural hue and a permanent frown plastered on its face.

Then a chill ran through him.

"It's not a doll," Lars stammered.

INSPECTOR MAGNUS Lund didn't learn about the man in the canal until long after he'd finished eating his breakfast.

Before he woke, his wife, Marta, had left for a teachers' conference in Gothenburg, a two hours' drive south of their home on the eastern shore of Lake Vänern.

Lund had planned to go into work after Marta returned from her trip. Maybe early afternoon. All he had to do was some paperwork. Maybe, by then, the workers would have finished moving his desk from the old stone police station behind the old theater in Mariestad's city center to the new low-slung office building next to the county lockup on the other side of the Tidan River.

Before the telephone rang, he had settled on the couch in the small living room to begin reading *Polis polis potatisgris,* the Martin Beck mystery published the year before. He had gotten about ten pages into the book when he was interrupted.

His mind was so focused on the murder at the Savoy Hotel in Malmo authors Maj Sjowall and Per Wahloo described at the start of their crime novel, Lund had to ask the caller to repeat herself.

"Where did you say the body was found?"

At first, her answer didn't make sense.

"In a lock on the canal at Norrkalm, you say?"

Lund put down his book, carefully placing a marker on the page where he'd left off, and asked the police dispatcher to repeat her report.

Before she was done, Lund had formulated his plan.

"Tell the superintendent, I will go to the scene," he told the dispatcher. "Please tell him he must send someone with a car to get me. My wife has taken our car for the morning, and I have no transportation."

After thanking the dispatcher for the call, Lund, a lanky man with short, graying hair, stretched out on the couch and resumed reading about Martin Beck, the fictional Swedish homicide detective

About ten pages later, Lund heard the rev of a powerful engine as an automobile pulled up to the small house, a former cottage in a small lakeside colony of summer camps about ten kilometers from Mariestad just off the road to Torso, the large island just north of the city.

Must be Gunderson, Lund surmised.

Before getting up from the couch, Lund placed his bookmark back between the pages. Retrieving the brown bag containing the lunch Marta had put up for him the night before from the refrigerator in the small galley kitchen, he walked out the front door of the bungalow to find Gunderson sitting behind the steering wheel, racing the engine of the large blue-and-white Dodge squad car.

After sliding into the passenger seat, Lund received his usual warm greeting from the young policeman. "Good morning, Max!"

Gunderson was convinced Lund resembled Max Von Sydow, the renowned Swedish actor. Like the actor, Lund was tall and thin.

However, his features were not as well-defined as Von Sydow's, whose face was capable of conveying a wide range of emotions. Lund's lean angular face always seemed to wear the same, slightly sardonic expression. It conveyed little emotion.

"Good morning, Ulf," was all Lund said. He never let on how he felt about the young policeman's pet name for him. It amused Lund, but he never showed it. Lund buckled in for the wild ride he knew was about to begin. "Do you know where we're going?"

While turning the steering wheel with one hand, Gunderson

tapped the side of his head with the index finger of his free hand. "Got the directions, right here." The young policeman spun the patrol car around in the narrow area in back of the cottage, throwing up a wide arc of gravel in its wake, and headed back toward the main road. "I know a shortcut."

As the car barreled down the dirt track toward the paved main road, Lund looked back to see whether the rocks thrown up by Gunderson's maneuver had hit any of the windows on his home. Seeing no apparent damage, the police inspector settled back in his seat and tried to enjoy the ride.

"I heard we got a floater," Gunderson said, gunning the engine after the patrol car reached the highway.

"Floater" wasn't a term Lund employed. However, it was probably an apt description.

"Yes, it sounds like another suicide," Lund said. "But you can never tell. We'll go out there and have a look, and we'll try to keep an open mind."

Keeping an open mind was paramount to Lund's approach to his work. In his cases, he continually sifted through the evidence, conducting a seemingly never-ending review, before arriving at a resolution. He tried not to jump to conclusions. He just patiently went about his business. His meticulous methodology drove some of his younger colleagues wild.

However, when it came to suicide in Sweden, Lund was well aware of the statistics. The small Scandinavian country had one of the highest suicide rates in the world. It was a national concern. Yet no one seemed able to do much about it. In fact, at some levels within the police hierarchy, there was pressure to sweep the issue under the rug.

Lund was sure some of the suicides which had occurred within his district had been incorrectly labeled as "accidents." It kept the official suicide rate down even more.

Lund knew of one instance where a husband had been arrested for murder after his wife was found hanging in the shower. An autopsy revealed the woman had also taken a handful of sleeping pills before she died. Apparently, she couldn't wait for the tablets to take effect. To speed up the job, she rigged up a noose from her nightgown. The grieving husband was released.

It took the two policemen less than fifteen minutes to reach the lock on the Göta Canal.

After cutting across the narrow, twisting road through a stand of birches toward Faleberg, Gunderson headed south down Route 26 past the old stone church to hook up with the E-3, the main highway between Gothenburg and Stockholm.

Traffic was light. But the young patrolman, as usual, buzzed past every car on the road, with his blue lights flashing and his klaxon blaring.

Just before reaching the drawbridge at Lyrstad, Gunderson turned right onto a narrow country lane that ran parallel to the canal through pastureland for about two kilometers before cutting back into the woods.

Moments later, they arrived at Norrkalm, a small village straddling the canal. Gunderson had to park the patrol car on the side of the road some distance from the lock.

"Where do all these people come from?" Gunderson muttered, as the two policemen trekked past the parked cars along the narrow country lane leading to the lock. "Do they live in the trees?"

"It's summer time, Ulf," Lund explained. "This is probably their first bit of excitement. Nothing ever happens here."

Dozens of people lined both sides of the canal.

The body was still floating in the murky water at the bottom of the lock. It had been nearly three hours since the two boys had awakened Samuelson. More than two hours had passed since the old lock keeper had reported their find to the police. Sometimes, news traveled slowly in Mariestad.

Minutes after the call came in, a local constable had arrived on the scene. For the past two hours, his main function was to keep a group of men who lived in the village from going into the lock to retrieve the body.

"I'm glad to see you, inspector," the constable said. He was a veteran policeman whom Lund knew well. "I've had to hold these people back from the canal. I didn't think anyone should touch the body before you arrived."

Lund looked down into the lock to see the bloated body nestled against the large wooden gate at the far end of the lock. Every once in a while a gentle breeze sent a ripple through the water in the bottom of the lock, and the corpse would gently bob against the door.

"Has the Coast Guard Service been alerted?" Lund asked.

"A boat from Gothenburg was out on the lake and it's on its way." The constable looked at his watch. "It should be here within the hour."

"Good," Lund responded. "We'll wait for the Coast Guard. They'll know what to do."

The removal of the body from the canal required special handling. Its bloated condition indicated the corpse had been submerged a long time. If not handled properly, the body could come apart as it was pulled from the water.

Lund didn't want anything to go wrong. The dead man's family would be appalled if his remains fell apart. Also, the man in the canal could be a murder victim. Some valuable evidence could be lost if the body disintegrated because it was mishandled.

The Coast Guard was trained to use the proper techniques, and Lund knew the crew on the boat motoring across Lake

Vänern had probably had a lot of experience pulling bodies out of the lake.

Waiting for the Coast Guard was a prudent move. However, because of the delay in the opening of the lock, it wasn't a popular one. Already, a long line of powerboats and sailboats extended along the canal waiting to move through the lock and resume their leisurely cruise through the beautiful Swedish countryside to Stockholm.

The constable told Lund he'd been fielding complaints ever since he arrived on the scene. "Samuelson, the lock keeper, got so fed up he went home. These people are pissed."

The corpse floated in a lock located about ten kilometers from the beginning of this section of the one-hundred-thirty-year-old canal. Earlier that morning, the boats had passed through a series of locks at the village of Sjotorp on the portion of the waterway leading from Lake Värnern, Sweden's largest lake, to the much smaller Lake Vixen.

The canal was built during the early nineteenth century to connect Sweden's two largest cities, Stockholm and Gothenburg. It took more than fifty-eight thousand men and more than twenty years to build it. However, a short time after its construction was completed, it was deemed obsolete because of the railroad. Subsequently, owners turned the canal, sometimes known as the Blue Ribbon of Sweden, into a tourist attraction.

As Lund looked at the long string of boats waiting to enter the lock, he noticed the M/S *Diana*, one of the fleet of three small passenger ships specially built to traverse the canal, among them. On board the miniature cruise ship, dozens of passengers, most of whom had paid thousands of krona to spend a leisurely week cruising through some of the most picturesque scenery in Sweden, were cooling their heels. They will just have to wait, he thought.

Lund would have to wait, too. While he did, he peered down into the eight-meter wide stone lock at the bloated corpse. The body, with its arms in a raised position gently floating behind its head, stared back at him with its large black vacant eyes.

It had all the appearances of a suicide, but there was one detail that just didn't look right to Lund.

Strange, he thought.

In his experience, after bodies bobbed back to the surface, most drowning victims floated face down in the water

The man in the canal floated on his back.

IT WAS NOON, and U.S. Army Criminal Investigation Division investigator John Murphy was exactly where he was supposed to be—standing alone beneath the arch of the historic Holstein Gate in the old German city of Lubeck.

That morning, Murphy had taken the short ride on the train from Hamburg. The day before, he'd entered West Germany after spending nearly a week touring the Low Countries, spending most of his time on the beaches in Belgium and Holland, building his cover.

Prior to leaving Fort Hamilton at the Brooklyn end of the Verrazano Narrows Bridge, he was told to spend some time traveling in Europe before arriving in Lubeck, where he'd learn the nature of his new undercover assignment.

"If anyone asks you what you're doing, tell them you're screwing your way through Europe," suggested the chief warrant officer who ran the CID detachment at Fort Hamilton.

While touring some of northern Europe's most beautiful beaches, Murphy really didn't try to follow that directive. Anyway, Murphy was nearly thirty, too old for the bikini-clad teeny boppers who populated the sandy beaches at Duinbergen and West Kapelle. At least, that's what he thought.

Besides, Murphy had someone waiting for him at home. Maybe. When he last saw Kate two weeks before, she was wasn't too happy with him.

"You're going away again?" she asked.

"Yes," he answered.

"And you can't tell me where you're going?"

"Not this time."

"And you can't tell me what you're doing?"

Murphy remembered shaking his head. "I don't know what I am doing."

Kate's voice went up another octave.

"This coming and going. This breezing in and out of my life." She shrugged her shoulders emphatically. "I don't know if I can handle it anymore."

Other women had delivered essentially the same message in the past. Murphy wondered whether the pretty nurse from South Boston, with a four-year-old son who seemed to worship him, would wait for him. He really didn't know.

As the minutes ticked by, Murphy wondered whether he had come to the correct location. With its twin cylindrical towers, the Holstein Gate was a distinctive landmark. From a distance, it resembled two ice cream cones turned upside down. It had to be the right place.

For fifteen minutes, Murphy slowly paced back and forth through the archway. On one side of the arch was a small, grassy park. It was lunchtime, and several office girls were sunbathing, feasting on the sun after removing their blouses and spreading blankets on the lawn.

"A pretty sight, huh?" Murphy heard someone say as he lingered to watch the show. "German girls sure love the sun."

Murphy turned to find a tall, thin man with sandy brown hair standing next to him, with his right arm extended in greeting.

"The name's Smith," he smiled, "and you must be John Murphy."

Another Smith. The world is full of them, thought Murphy.

Three years before, upon his arrival in Ethiopia, of all places, a man with a similar last name provided Murphy with a passport for another undercover assignment. He'd used it on this trip to Europe.

When traveling overseas in uniform, Murphy carried the red-covered passport normally used by employees of the federal government on official business. These days, he seldom went anywhere in his uniform. With his long hair and goatee, Murphy really didn't look like he belonged in one.

Smith apologized. "Sorry I'm late." He placed a friendly hand on Murphy's shoulder while guiding him through the arch into the small park. The pair looked like two old friends. "I had to drive down from Travemunde. The traffic is murder this time of day. I left the missus on the beach, ogling some German hunks. She thinks we're on vacation."

In a small grove of trees, not far from where one of the pretty sunbathers lay on a blanket stripped down to her bra and panties, the two men found a metal park bench. Close by, the raunchy beat of T-Rex's "Get It On" emanated from a transistor radio. Immediately after the two men sat down, Smith got down to business. From the thin briefcase he carried, he removed a large manila envelope and handed it to Murphy.

"Mr. Murphy, you're going to Sweden," he announced. "Open the envelope, please. Look at the picture."

The envelope contained an enlargement of a military identification photo. From the buzz cut the soldier wore, Murphy assumed it had been taken during basic training. Aside from the haircut, none of the soldier's features were distinctive. Everything about him was average. Eyes. Ears. Nose. Mouth. Everything went together. It was a picture of someone who could easily get lost in a crowd.

"What am I supposed to do with this? Eat it?" Murphy offered the portrait to Smith. "You might as well pencil in a beard and a mustache."

Smith was apologetic. He sounded like it was a habit. "It's not much help, I know." He pointed at the photo. "But let me tell you a little bit about our friend here."

After removing a sheath of papers from his briefcase, Smith

launched into his monologue: "His name is Marlon Andrews. But his friends call him Fish. Born in Chalfont, Pennsylvania, March 3, 1948. Drafted into the United States Army June 7, 1969. He's a smart boy, so he was sent to Army finance school at Fort Benjamin Harrison in Indianapolis. Finished at the top of his class and, at his request, was assigned to the headquarters of a mechanized infantry outfit down near Bad Kreuznach. While at B.K., he got involved in drugs in a big way, dealing marijuana, some hash. After his discharge, he stayed in West Germany. He's a bad actor. We think he knocked off a soldier who was trying to horn in on his operation, and then took off. We want you to find him."

When the briefing ended, Murphy studied the photograph for a time, trying to picture what Andrews looked like with a full head of long hair, and perhaps a beard or a mustache. Hell, he could look like me, it occurred to him.

"What makes you think he went to Sweden?"

"A lot of our guys have gone to Sweden lately," Smith said. "There's more than a thousand soldiers, sailors, marines and airmen who have deserted and gone up there. None of them want to go to Nam. Fish is no deserter, but we think he's hiding out among them."

After a brief pause, Smith added: "We tracked him to Denmark. We know he entered the country, but there's no record of him leaving. The Danish cops are very thorough, and they believe he's no longer there. He likes to be with his own kind. There's lots of Americans in Sweden, and it's just a twenty-minute ferry ride from Copenhagen to Malmo."

Murphy slid the picture back into the envelope.

"This isn't going to be much help," he said. "Got anything else?"

Smith shook his head. "Apparently, our man didn't think he

was very photogenic. Other than that, we have zip." Smith lev-
eled an appraising look at Murphy. "But he's about your size and
nearly as tall, pushing six feet."

Murphy stood nearly six feet tall and weighed a muscular two
hundred pounds.

"And there's one other thing," said Smith, turning to show
the inside of his right wrist to Murphy. "There's a scar." With the
index finger of his left hand, he drew an imaginary line. "Right
here, on his wrist. Very distinctive, I'm told."

Murphy looked at Smith's wrist.

"Shrapnel?" he asked. "In Vietnam?"

Smith shook his head. "Our boy didn't go to Nam, remember? No, it was a box cutter at a Safeway."

"Safeway?"

"Before Andrews was drafted, he worked as a stock boy at a
supermarket. One day he was opening some cardboard boxes
for an end display, and he got careless." Smith redrew the line
on his wrist. "Twenty stitches, right here."

With that, Smith reached into his briefcase and removed a
stack of cash. "There's a couple of grand here." He handed the
money to Murphy. "German marks. Swedish krona. British ster-
ling. American greenbacks. Small bills, mostly. Go up there and
spread it around."

Got a problem? Throw some money at it, thought Murphy. It's
the American Way.

Murphy shoved the wad of money into the inside pocket of
his old Army field jacket. "So I'm bait, huh?"

Another nod. "If there's one thing Andrews likes, and probably
needs a lot of right now, it's money," Smith said. "Most of our boys go
to Sweden flat broke. They got to work to survive, and, if there's one
thing Andrews is not into, it's work. No, he's always looking to score.
He'll look for some easy money. You can count on it."

It wasn't an easy assignment, which was consistent with the cases Murphy had been working lately.

Just prior to coming to Europe, Murphy had spent time on the streets of New York and Philadelphia trying to track down the connection between the local drug lords and a ring of soldiers dealing pot, hash and acid to the troops at Fort Dix, the large Army base in south New Jersey.

Now, he was supposed to find a man for whom he had a scant physical description, whose only distinctive physical feature was a scar on his right wrist, living among eight million Swedes.

At least in New York and Philadelphia, everyone spoke the same language. Sort of.

"Why me?" Murphy asked. "Surely, you got CID agents over here who can go look for this guy."

The comment rated another apologetic look.

"None of the CID agents we got over here can get close to this guy," Smith explained. "They stand out like sore thumbs. But someone like you will fit right in. Christ, you look like a hippie!"

Another pat on Murphy's shoulder.

"Why did you think we met like this? Driving over here, I did two or three cutouts to make sure I wasn't tailed," Smith went on.

"These deserters have got a whole network. They know all of us. Besides, all of the CID investigators we have in Sweden are busy trying to get these guys to come back. We tell them, 'come home, all is forgiven.' But actually, Uncle Sam wants to read them the riot act."

Murphy had a question. "If I do find him, what do I do about it? I can't just haul his ass out of Sweden, can I?"

Smith handed him a white business card. Except for the handwritten telephone number on it, it was blank.

"Call this number, day or night, and we'll come and get you,"

Smith said. "Just find the guy." He followed up with a question of his own. "You got your credentials on you?"

Murphy reached across his body with his left hand and patted the First Cav shoulder patch on the right sleeve of the old Army field jacket he wore.

"Right, here," he said.

Murphy had sewn his ID card under the large black-and-yellow patch. Because of the size and thickness of the black horse patch, he was sure the little plastic card with his picture on it would escape detection during a pat down.

The left shoulder bore the distinctive shield worn by soldiers assigned to units within the Military District of Washington. At its center was a replica of the Washington Monument.

Originally, the jacket was worn by a Corporal Beeman, the name on the tag above the right-hand breast pocket. Since the Washington District shoulder patch didn't include the red Honor Guard slash above it, Murphy guessed Beeman, whoever he was, was assigned to a dick job at Fort Myers or Fort McNair after putting in a much harder twelve months in Vietnam. However, there was no Combat Infantryman's Badge above the left breast pocket.

The year before, Murphy bought the jacket for fifteen dollars at an Army surplus store in Boston. His Army-issue field jacket, crisp and clean, hung in his wall locker in the barracks at Fort Hamilton.

For the past year, Murphy had worn Beeman's jacket every time he hit the streets. He had spilled food on it, rolled in the grease and grime of back alleys in Philadelphia, New York and Boston while trying to subdue suspects. It had never been washed. The jacket looked faded and soiled, exactly how Murphy wanted it to look.

Smith made a final assessment.

"You look like a bum," he stated.

Murphy shrugged his shoulders and smiled.

"With that fat bankroll of yours, I'm sure the Swedes will still let you in."

WHEN AT HOME the Lunds normally spoke English. Marta taught English in the school at Mariestad, and the conversations helped her remain proficient in her second language, especially during the summer months when she was out of the classroom.

The practice also was good for Lund. After all, it never hurt to be able to speak a language other than your own.

Sometimes, the Lunds would read the same books in English at the same time—their bookmarks leapfrogging over each other as they went along. Then, they'd sit down and discuss what they had read. In English.

However, when Lund was upset or excited, he often lapsed into Svenska. Tonight, it seemed every other word was in his native tongue.

"What's the matter?" Marta asked. In English. She was a tall, auburn-haired woman, with a pretty face easily capable of registering emotion.

At the moment, she wore a look of concern.

The couple sat on the couch. Through one of the large picture windows which Lund had installed in the front of the former summer retreat, they could see the waters of Lake Vänern extending into the ever-reddening western horizon.

Pooling their savings, the Lunds purchased the camp shortly after they were married. For years they had lived in an apartment in Mariestad, in the cobblestone old town section in front of the monolithic cathedral which dominated the town's skyline. The couple scrimped and saved before accumulating enough money to winterize and expand the cottage.

18

Most evenings, they made sure they were home with each other. It was a time for them to talk.

"I think I might have a case," Lund told her.

"Is that bad?" Marta was well aware of the type of cases her husband usually worked on. Petty theft. Stolen cars. The occasional assault. In a small city like Mariestad, where everybody knew everybody else, there were few secrets. Normally, those crimes were easily solved, not much of a challenge for Lund. When her husband used the word "case," Marta knew it meant something more substantial. A real mystery.

Lund told her about the man in the canal.

"Gunderson and I had to wait until the coast guard came around noon before we got a good look at the body," he said. "We haven't got a clue how it got there. Probably dragged into the lock by one of the boats. It looked like it had been in the water for a long time."

Lund didn't elaborate. His wife didn't need to know all of the details.

Marta, her long legs stretched out in front of the divan, continued to gaze at the horizon, with its varying shades of purple coloring the clouds out over the lake. "You don't think it's a suicide?"

Her husband nodded. "An accident, maybe."

Lund described how the body floated on its back inside the canal lock. "Most drowning victims float face down."

Marta, who was wearing shorts, swiveled in her perch to face her husband. "So, you think it is murder."

Lund turned to face her. "Maybe."

Not that the police inspector had much experience investigating murders.

Suicides, yes. Murders, no.

Sweden had one of the world's highest suicide rates, but its murder rate ranked among its lowest.

"So you might have a real mystery on your hands," Marta said.

Lund nodded slightly.

None of the few murders Lund had investigated during his twenty-year career as a policeman could be termed "mysteries." All had been open-and-shut cases. Usually, the crimes involved alcohol, a heated argument between friends or acquaintances, sometimes a husband and a wife, and ready access to a fire-arm, knife or a heavy blunt object.

"When will you know?" Marta asked.

"The body was taken to the hospital in Mariestad." Lund, calm now, spoke strictly in English. "Doctor Gustavson said he would perform the autopsy tomorrow morning. I should know sometime in the afternoon."

From his manner, Marta could tell her husband was itching to start an investigation. Since the Swedish police were nation-alized in 1965, that wasn't always possible. The really tough murder cases, the particularly heinous crimes that resulted in headlines in the national press, were usually assigned to the National Criminal Investigation Department. Local investigators often took a back seat to "The Boys From Stockholm," and this case looked like it might fall into that category.

"Has anyone been called in?"

"Not yet." After turning on the light on the end table next to where he was sitting, Lund picked up the mystery novel he had started reading that morning. "We just don't know enough yet. Hopefully, tomorrow, Gustavson will be able to provide a cause of death as well as the identity of the poor fellow."

"It sounds like you might be busy," Marta observed. After a slight pause, she added: "You know we have company coming."

Lund knew.

It was July, start of the traditional vacation period in Sweden. It was a time when a lot of Swedes headed for cottages on the lakes in the southern part of the country to swim or sail, or they went to camp in the forests in the northern region to hunt, fish or hike.

Usually, at this time of year, Marta's sister, Anita, and her husband, Peter, and their two children, Arvid and Britta, came down from their home in Stockholm to spend a week with the Lunds. The Nillsons were scheduled to arrive in two days.

Lund especially looked forward to the visits from his niece and nephew. He and Marta had no children of their own. By chance, not by choice. He enjoyed having the two youngsters around. The pair seemed content to spend most of their time traipsing behind their Uncle Magnus.

Normally, Lund took time off to spend time with his relatives. Now he might have to change his plans

As Marta gently reminded him, there was more. "You and Peter had planned to work on the sauna together, remember?"

Lund nodded. "I know."

Absently, he began fiddling with the bookmark.

The sauna had been a project in the planning stages ever since Peter, a finance banker who happened to be very handy with tools, and Lund had finished renovating the cottage. Over the course of several summers, the two men had completed the conversion of the little seasonal cottage into a year-round residence.

With its shed-like roof, the house retained the lines of a traditional Swedish cottage. However, an ell had been added to the rear of the structure, away from the narrow sandy beach.

The Lunds slept in a small bedroom in the original part of the cottage, which also included a galley kitchen, a small bath and the sitting room looking out over the lake. Guests slept in the open room in the ell.

The cottage was not massive. In Sweden, because of the cost to heat in the long, cold winters, most homes were built on a small scale. However, there was plenty of room for everybody, and its tidy design had a comfortable feel to it.

Since they were first married, Marta had wanted a sauna of her own.

Now, it appeared the construction of the small sweat house would have to be postponed, or at least slowed. Lund wasn't happy with that prospect. "I'm sorry, Marta. I don't know what to say. But if this is a murder case, I must start right off. It can't wait."

Removing her clogs, Marta slid a little closer to Lund. "I understand," she said.

Lund opened the book to the page he had marked. "Maybe, Peter and I can work something out. Maybe, he can start without me."

Lund held the book in front of him to resume reading. However, before he could remove the bookmark, Marta's bare foot nudged his slippered feet. He looked over to his wife.

Marta smiled coyly. "Aren't you coming to bed?"

Lund looked down at his book.

Then, he glanced back at his wife.

The smile was still there.

Lund closed the book and put it back where he found it.

THE MORNING after his meeting with Smith, Murphy boarded the auto ferry *Nil Holgersson* for the eight-hour voyage from Travemunde to Trelleborg on Sweden's southern tip.

The early-morning haze, which rolled in off the Baltic Sea obscuring the famed beaches of the German resort, had burned off, revealing a cloudless blue sky.

The night before, Murphy had splurged, laying out fifty German marks for a room in a cozy inn within walking distance of the beach.

However, Murphy didn't spend any time lolling in the sand. Unsure of what lay ahead, what kind of demands would be placed on his mind and body, he ate well and got plenty of rest.

After a dinner of roast duck, served Lubeck style with a brandy-laced, sweet-tasting stuffing, Murphy slept well. For breakfast, the innkeeper had served up a large stack of hotcakes, filled with raisins and currants.

As the *Holgersson* got underway, Murphy felt refreshed, eager to take on his new assignment. As sea voyages go, the trip from Travemunde to Trelleborg was brief. But it was long enough for Murphy to reflect on his mission. Too long.

While standing on the deck in the bow of the auto ferry, he wondered how he would complete his assignment. It was much too early for him to formulate a plan. Hopefully, it would evolve once he got his feet on the ground in Stockholm.

Getting his bearings in Sweden could take some time. He'd never been to Scandinavia before. He didn't speak the language. As far as he knew, Andrews didn't speak the language either. Like Smith said, Murphy was looking for someone just like himself.

It wasn't the first time the Army had sent Murphy out on his own on a seemingly impossible mission. Three years before, he'd been sent to Ethiopia. There, he worked undercover to find the murderer of a soldier at Kagnew Station, a U.S. military installation. That case had been resolved to everyone's satisfaction but his own.

It had left a bad taste, and Murphy wondered whether this case would end just as sourly.

For the first hour of the cruise across the Baltic, Murphy had the bow of the *Holgersson* all to himself. It was peaceful. Aside from the low rumble of the ferry's diesel engines and the whoosh of the spray from the ship's bow as it sliced through the water, there was no sound. The setting was almost serene, with just a hint of a breeze caused by the boat's movement through the slight chop.

Murphy's mind drifted. He thought of Kate.

She wasn't happy when he told her he was leaving for an assignment in Europe. Kate never liked it when he went away. Sometimes before he left for an undercover assignment, Murphy would go for three or four days without shaving. That was always a tip off.

The atmosphere grew cold.

Sometimes, during his undercover assignments in New York or Philadelphia, Murphy would take a chance and call her. It didn't help. His calls were not greeted with warmth. A barrier would go up between them.

Now, Murphy was traveling in Europe for who knows how long. This time, he couldn't even tell her exactly where he was going. Until Smith told him, he didn't know. It only made it worse.

During the three days he spent in Amsterdam, Murphy had bought a post card featuring one of its famed canals. He wanted to write "Wish you here" on the back and send it to Kate.

But Murphy knew he wasn't supposed to tell her where "here" was. Not at that point in the mission. The postcard remained in his backpack, with no address, unsigned and with no personal message. It became another piece of his cover.

Murphy understood Kate's reaction. Tommy, her four-year-old son, had become attached to him. Early on, Kate told Murphy she didn't want to be involved with a man who walked in and out of her life.

Tommy already had enough of that, Murphy knew.

According to Kate, the boy's father had drifted off, in a haze of marijuana. They never married. He was never around.

But the guy tried to stay connected. Sometimes he worked road construction up in Maine. In the summers, when there was lots of work, he'd send Kate money to help. In the winters, when construction jobs were scarce, he'd draw unemployment and Kate wouldn't get a cent. Not that she needed the money. Kate was a nurse. She could take care of herself and Tommy. The checks Tommy's father sent went into a separate bank account for his son. When he got older, she would let Tommy decide what do about his father's money.

Murphy understood why Kate felt the way she did. He knew what it was like to grow up without a father. His dad was killed while serving with the army in the South Pacific during World War II a short time after Murphy's birth. His mother raised him on her own. Often, she told Murphy she never met anyone who could replace his father in her heart. It was a void that couldn't be filled. It was a void he shared.

Since getting to know Kate and her son, Murphy had thought about leaving the army. But he didn't know whether he could stop being a detective. At least not cold turkey. He considered getting a job with the Boston Police Department. His two uncles, his mother's younger brothers, were now both senior detectives.

They had some sway. Anyway, serving with the Boston PD was the business of a lot of Massachusetts families.

Surely, Murphy had enough experience for that kind of work. But after nearly twelve years in the Army, he wasn't sure he was ready to leave that life. He enjoyed working undercover. It gave him a chance to think on his feet, and, truth be told, he still got a rush out of it.

Murphy reached for a cigarette. The wind out on the deck was negligible, but he had a difficult time getting his Zippo to work. Just before he left the states he had added lighter fluid. Maybe, it was the flint. Murphy hadn't replaced that in a while.

Then, Murphy's thoughts returned to his assignment, which is where he knew his mind should be.

This case was different.

Murphy had been on his own before, but usually there was someone nearby to watch his back. For much of his time in Vietnam, where Murphy worked undercover in a signal unit for a couple of months, it was Van Dyck, an old CID warrant officer.

Three years before, while on that brief assignment in Ethiopia, Smyth, the mysterious man from the American consulate in Asmara, was always a phone call away. Murphy was in the country only for five days, but he managed to make a friend, Romana. She provided him with valuable support.

Funny, Murphy recalled, Romana was a nurse, too. So was Michelle, another pretty nurse who dumped him during his second tour in Vietnam. What was it with nurses?

Murphy never wondered what happened to Michelle. At first, the breakup, or the way she coldly informed him in a letter she sent while he was in Vietnam, stung him. But after a while, he realized she had done him a favor.

The end of his friendship with Romana was different. She indicated she wanted to remain in touch with him when she gave him her mailing address on the day he left Asmara. Murphy wrote her once at that address. Then, at her direction, he began writing to her through one of her American friends at Kagnew Station. They exchanged letters infrequently for nearly a year until Romana, without any warning, stopped writing him. Murphy even sent a note to Smyth at the consulate to find out whether anything had happened to her, but that query went unanswered. Murphy suspected Romana's American friend had left Kagnew Station for another duty station. When Romana lost her link to him, she stopped writing. But he really didn't know what happened.

For the past two years, while on undercover assignments in Boston, New York or Philadelphia, Murphy usually worked as part of a team. He seldom worked alone.

This time, Murphy was on his own. What's more, he had scant information. Just a name and a physical description that was probably out of date. Not much to go on. But Murphy really didn't have to do much.

All the CID investigator had to do was to find Marlon Andrews. Pin him down. Then call in the cavalry. Simple.

For a moment, Murphy thought about Van Dyck. What would he do about his problem? The one he had with women. Not about his assignment in Sweden. "Love 'em and leave 'em" would be V.D.'s advice. That's for sure, thought Murphy.

It had been nearly four years since Van Dyck had been killed. At first, Murphy had thought about his old partner all the time. "What would Van Dyck do?" he'd asked himself. As time went on, it happened less and less. Still, Murphy's last memory of V.D., as he was called, never went away.

Suddenly, Murphy realized he wasn't alone. His reveries ceased.

A few feet away, further back from the bow, a man stood,

clinging to the thick cable which served as the ship's railing, staring out at the water.

After flicking his third cigarette of the morning into the sea, Murphy stepped toward his fellow passenger, a compactly-built man much younger than himself.

"You *sprecken* the English?"

Murphy's question was answered with a slight southern twang. "I sure do."

However, no smile accompanied what was an otherwise friendly reply to Murphy's query. Instead, the young, boyish face wore a troubled look.

From the accent, as well as his blue jeans and the Mountaineers sweatshirt worn under his light poplin jacket, Murphy deduced the young man was an American. From his short haircut and clean-shaven face, he guessed he was a soldier.

"You on leave?" Murphy asked.

The young man's troubled expression grew even more wide-eyed.

"Not, not, not exactly," he stammered, looking away.

Murphy took out the pack of Rothmans he had purchased at the inn before he left. He figured the hard-drawing filtered cigarette would help him kick the habit. So far, it hadn't help. He seemed to be smoking even more.

"You want a smoke?" Murphy asked, holding the flat cigarette box out to the young man.

"Thanks," he said, sounding relieved as he took a cigarette.

Murphy offered his right hand in greeting. "John Murphy, here."

The young man shook his hand. "Ricky. Ricky Conrad," he mumbled.

His grip was weak.

Something is not right here, Murphy sensed.

"So, what have you got? A weekend pass?"

Conrad answered that question with one of his own. "How did you know I was in the Army?"

Murphy gave Conrad an appraising look. "From your haircut." Then, Murphy touched his own unshaven face. "No beard." Then, he pointed to the sweatshirt. "And your clothes."

In marked contrast, Murphy wore his dark hair long, well over his ears. He also wore a goatee. However, the three-day-old growth on the rest of his cheeks and neck gave him a swarthy look. Distinctly unmilitary.

Averting his eyes, Conrad appeared to take stock of himself. "Yeah, I could see why it could be easy to tell."

Murphy pulled out his Zippo. It took several flicks of the thumb wheel before he was able to light cigarettes for both of them.

"Well, which is it?" he asked. "Are you on leave? Or is it a three-day pass?"

Conrad took a long drag. "Neither," he stated. "I'm going to Sweden to desert."

While taking a long drag on his cigarette, Murphy stifled a cough.

"Desert?" It wasn't a question. Murphy couldn't believe what he'd just heard.

Conrad nodded. "The Army wants to send me to Vietnam, and I don't want to go."

Murphy regained his composure. "That's an awfully big step." He looked Conrad in the eye. "You sure you want to do this?"

Another nod. "I've been thinking about this ever since I joined the Army. I know it's a big step, but it's one I got to take."

Conrad told Murphy he enlisted in the Army less than two years before, after he drew a low number in the draft lottery following his graduation from high school in West Virginia. He decided to pick his poison, he said, rather than have the Army pick one for him.

At the suggestion of his recruiter, Conrad became a lithographer. Following training at Fort Meade in Maryland, he was sent to Germany, where he operated an offset printing press for an armored brigade.

"My recruiter lied to me," he said. "Because of the troop withdrawals, he said I wouldn't have to go to Vietnam. He told me there was little need there for guys with my MOS."

Murphy played dumb. "What's an MOS?"

"It's your military occupation specialty," Conrad said. "I'm an 83C20, a letter pressman."

About a month before, Conrad received orders for Vietnam.

"I got assigned as a replacement to the 101st Airborne in I Corps, up near the DMZ," he said.

Murphy was quite familiar with that territory. He'd spent time up in Thua Thien province, not far from the DMZ. But he didn't let on.

"When my orders came through, I went to my CO to see if there was anything he could do about it," Conrad continued. "He said his hands were tied."

Once he got started, Conrad couldn't stop talking. It all poured out.

"I ain't scared of dying," he stated. "I just don't see any good about dying in Vietnam. The only reason I joined the Army was because I was going to get drafted anyway. But I didn't want to carry a rifle."

Conrad claimed he arrived at his decision to become a deserter after a lot of soul-searching. It wasn't easy.

"If he knew what I was doing, my granddaddy would be rolling over in his grave," he said. "Conrads have been going to war ever since the Civil War."

Murphy wondered which side the Conrads had fought on.

"When my daddy finds out, he'll want to kill me," Conrad added. "He won't like it, but I'm pretty sure I'm doing the right thing."

If the situation was different, Murphy would be slapping the cuffs on Conrad and marching him off to the nearest provost marshal's office.

Bringing in deserters was not part of this mission.

Finding Marlon Andrews was.

"Why Sweden?" Murphy asked.

Conrad seemed completely at ease as he continued to explain himself to Murphy.

"I talked to some of my buddies. One of them told me he knew somebody from our outfit who took off to Sweden before I got to Germany. He gave me the guy's address, and I wrote him. A German friend of mine mailed the letter for me. He wrote me back and told me what to do."

The network Smith talked about, Murphy thought.

"Someone is supposed to meet me," Conrad said. "He'll take me to Stockholm."

Murphy also wanted to go to Stockholm. That's where he intended to start his search for Andrews or Fish or whatever he was calling himself these days.

Abruptly, Conrad told Murphy he had to find a latrine. "I don't feel good." He clutched his stomach. "I think I'm going to throw up." The young soldier left the deck looking for the nearest head.

Murphy grew up on Cape Cod, where he often took the ferries out to Nantucket or Martha's Vineyard. The gentle roll of the *Holgersson* didn't bother him. He'd weathered rougher seas, even on the short runs out to the islands. However, it might be different for a landlubber like Conrad. For all Murphy knew, it might be the young Army deserter's first time aboard a ship.

After Conrad left, Murphy lit another cigarette. While he

smoked, he wondered what Van Dyck would make of the young soldier's story.

V.D. had gone to Vietnam.

But he never came back.

Murphy recalled conversations he'd had with the infantry veteran during the days just before he was killed.

Van Dyck had voiced concerns about the United States' involvement in the war, but he never questioned the Army's authority to send him to Vietnam.

As for Conrad?

Van Dyck might give him a pass. He was known to do that on occasion.

"I wouldn't want someone like him in my outfit, anyway," the old warrant officer would say. "Couldn't trust him to watch my back."

Murphy didn't intend to let Conrad watch his back.

Nor did the CID investigator want to take the troubled young man into custody.

At least not yet.

INSPECTOR LUND finally caught up with Doctor Gustavson late in the afternoon.

His day started with an investigation of a fire at the Domkyrkan, the cathedral that loomed over Mariestad's north end. Built in the sixteenth century, the cathedral was an exact duplicate of the church on Riddarholmen, the island in Stockholm where Sweden's nobility once lived. The same architect designed both churches. His patrons were princes, rival brothers contending for royal hegemony.

The brother in Stockholm won that battle, and the city on the coast became the seat of Swedish government. Although the world headquarters of Electrolux was now located in Mariestad, it became a political backwater, a small town with a large Gothic church that was now merely one of the region's primary tourist attractions.

At about ten o'clock, a visitor noticed smoke pouring from behind the huge pipe organ in the choir loft at the rear of the nearly five hundred-year-old landmark.

By the time Lund arrived, firemen had been on the scene for about twenty minutes. The fire started in a box of cleaning rags stored in a small closet. Although some of the lacquer on the woodwork had puckered in the heat from the small fire, none of it caught fire. However, the residue from the cleaning solvents on the rags produced a lot of smoke. Firemen had set up a series of fans to clear the air from the cathedral.

It was a case of arson, and it didn't take long for Lund to learn who set the fire. Before he arrived on the scene, one of the firemen had already fingered the culprit. The arsonist was easy to find.

During the summer months, tourists flocked to Mariestad to enjoy the nearby beaches. While firemen hustled in and out of the building ferrying equipment to the scene of the fire, a lot of people had walked up the hill from the city center to gawk. A sizable crowd had congregated across the street from the church. One man especially caught the eye of one of the young firemen, and he told his fire captain about him.

It took Lund less than five minutes to walk from the old police station, located on Nygatan behind the Theatro, through the business district, across the shady esplanade and up cobblestoned Kyrkogatan to the church.

When Lund arrived, the fire captain took him aside. "Look at that fellow over there." Discreetly, he pointed to a man standing at the head of the small knot of people closest to the massive church door. "Look at the grin on his face. He looks like he's going to have an orgasm."

Lund had to admit the expression on the man's face looked out of place. Most onlookers wore a confounded look of curiosity. However, this man, who was dressed casually in slacks and a zippered, lightweight jacket and appeared to be in his thirties, looked like he was about to achieve nirvana.

"I guess I'll have to talk to him," Lund said.

Before the smoke was cleared from the cathedral, Lund walked back down the hill to the police station with the prime arson suspect by his side.

The man, who turned out to be a vacationing fireman from Gothenburg, came peaceably. During the five-minute walk, he confessed to the crime.

When the fire captain came to the police station, he wasn't surprised to learn of the arsonist's profession. "I swear half of the men in my brigade are pyromaniacs. I hope you throw the book at him."

Then, almost as an afterthought, the fire captain asked: "What's his name?"

Lund looked on the intake form he was typing. "His name is Soumi. Into Soumi."

"Strange name for a Swedish fireman," the captain observed. "Sounds Finnish."

Lund nodded. "It's what the Finns call themselves. Soumi. It means the people."

It took the police inspector the rest of morning to complete the paperwork for the arrest. Much of the Mariestad police department already had moved one kilometer away to the new building across the Tidan River. Lund ended up walking across the small stone bridge, with Soumi at his side, to file the arrest papers. The new police office was located next to the county lockup, where the confessed arsonist would be housed until transport could be arranged to bring him to a facility near his home in the southwestern part of the country for a mental health evaluation.

It was an open-and-shut case.

However, the man in the canal was a different matter.

It wasn't a case of suicide.

It was a case of murder.

After walking two kilometers back across town, past the iconic stone *Bibliotheque* on leafy Dottninggatan, to the hospital, Lund sat through another of Doctor Gustavson's lengthy briefings before he learned what happened.

"As you can imagine, from the condition the body was found in, it wasn't easy to establish the cause of death," the pathologist stated at the outset.

As the two men and the pathologist's female assistant stood around the corpse that lay on a metal examining table, Gustavson continued.

"Quite early on, I was able to eliminate drowning as the cause of death," he said. "I found no water in the lungs nor in the stomach."

Lund understood what the absence of water in those organs meant.

It explained why the body floated on its back in the canal. Normally, the additional weight of water in the lungs and stomach prevented a corpse in the water from rolling over onto its back when it floated to the surface.

After glancing at the cadaver, which lay underneath a white sheet, the police inspector turned toward Gustavson. "So he was dead before he went into the water?"

The pathologist nodded. "Exactly, Magnus."

"An accident, perhaps?"

Gustavson, a dark, wiry man who spoke with a quiet intensity, shook his head. "In my examination, I found no evidence of head trauma." This man didn't hit his head, die and fall into the water. I also was able to eliminate heart attack or stroke. The man was relatively young, between the ages of twenty-five and thirty, and in good health right up until the moment he died."

Lund wondered when the pathologist was going to get to the point. He tried to speed up the process. "Then how did he die?"

With a grand gesture, Gustavson removed the sheet from the corpse. It was not a pretty sight. The swelling had subsided. However, the coloring of the body ranged from deep purple to a mottled brown. Incisions made by the pathologist during his examination crisscrossed the torso.

"As you can see, Magnus, coloration made it difficult for me to find where the bullet had entered the body," Gustavson stated.

"Bullet?"

"Exactly."

Using a large set of forceps especially designed for autopsies, the pathologist gently pulled the corpse's left arm away from the body. He pointed to the armpit.

"The bullet entered here, in between the eighth and ninth rib," he explained. "It passed through the left lung, the left ventricle, the right atrium. It sliced through the right pulmonary vein, and glanced off the sixth rib before exiting the body on the right side. Death was nearly instantaneous."

The pathologist moved around the table to stand behind his assistant, a pretty blonde who Lund thought looked out of place in such a morbid environment. Stepping behind her, Gustavson mumbled a few words to her.

Obediently, the young woman raised both of her arms and placed her hands behind her head. The balding pathologist, who was several inches shorter than his pretty assistant, disappeared from view. However, he kept on talking. "The killer merely stepped up, placed the muzzle here," Gustavson pointed the forceps inches away from the woman's exposed underarm. "And pulled the trigger like so."

The pathologist moved away from his assistant. "That would explain why the arms were found in the raised position. I had a devil of a time putting his arms back by his sides. Very ticklish situation."

Lund took out the small pad of paper he carried and scribbled a note. "Do you know the caliber of the murder weapon?"

"Unfortunately, no," Gustavson answered. "But I would say the killer was left-handed, or at least ambidextrous."

After making a notation, Lund asked: "Do you know the approximate time of death?"

That question drew a slight chuckle from Gustavson. "Unfortunately, no. But I might be able to give you the month in which the murder occurred."

"Month?"

"Exactly."

The pathologist pointed to the dead man's left leg. "See that purplish ring around the ankle there." Again, he used the large set of forceps to point. Lund bent over to examine the wide purplish line on the corpse's left ankle.

Gustavson showed Lund a piece of rope that had been tied to the body's left leg. "Common, everyday hemp." He draped the rope across the dead man's legs for a moment. "Originally, the body was weighted when it went into the water. The knot unraveled, and the corpse bobbed to the surface."

The pathologist estimated the body had been in the water perhaps four or five months. "It was deep, so the relatively cold temperatures at the bottom of the canal retarded decomposition. Of course, the epidermis is like a sponge. That's why the body was so bloated."

Lund did the calculations. That would mean the murder took place during the months of March or April.

"Do you know who the man is?"

Reluctantly it seemed, the pathologist shook his head. "Not yet."

Then, his mood seemed to brighten. "But I did a get a partial fingerprint from one of his thumbs. I sent it to Stockholm for identification. But I don't think it will be of much help."

Lund was puzzled. "Why do you say that?"

The pathologist moved back to Lund's side of the table. "There may not be any record of him in Stockholm. I don't think he was Swedish. I think he was an American."

"Really?" Lund studied the body for a few moments. "And what makes you think he was an American."

Gustavson pointed to a small tattoo on the left biceps of the corpse. Nearly washed out from discoloration and the months in the water, it was barely visible. However, Lund could see the outlines of a faded Globe and Anchor. He was not familiar with the symbol.

Gustavson filled him in. "I think the man in the canal used to be a member of the United States Marine Corps. The Globe and Anchor is the symbol for their Marines."

It took a few moments for Lund to digest this bit of information.

"An American Marine, you say?"

Gustavson beamed. "Exactly."

Lund moved on. "Do you have anything else for me?"

Gustavson shook his head. "Not today. But maybe tomorrow."

The pathologist explained: "As you can imagine, his clothes were sodden, and we had to be extremely careful when we removed them from the body. We didn't want to peel the skin off with it, so we cut it off in strips. We don't dare put them into a dryer because there might be some items in the pockets of his pants and jacket that would help identify him. So we're letting them dry naturally. It takes time."

Before he left, Lund asked whether Gustavson had filed a report with the NCID in Stockholm.

"Not yet, Magnus. Not until I've completed my work."

"Good," is all Lund said.

ABOUT A HALF HOUR BEFORE the *Nils Holgersson* was scheduled to dock in Trelleborg, a pilot came aboard to guide the auto ferry through the shoals.

A uniformed customs official also climbed aboard the ship. He was accompanied by a tall, thin red-haired man. After taking a brief look at the cars and lorries in the ship's hold, the two men made their way up the inside passageway to the large cabin on the ship's main deck.

As the *Holgersson* neared the Swedish coast, the passengers, mostly young German couples on holiday with their children in tow, left the main cabin to catch their first glimpse of Scandinavia.

However, several people, including Murphy and Conrad, remained inside. At one table in a corner of the large cabin, several truck drivers played cards. Not far from that group sat three teen-aged girls eyeing them.

In the middle of the room, Conrad sat moaning with his head on a table. Murphy sat in a chair across from him.

As soon as the customs official stepped into the room, Murphy noticed him. Within seconds, after surveying the room, the official made a beeline for Murphy's table.

"I'm looking for Richard Conrad," he stated when he reached the table. His English was slightly accented.

Murphy pointed toward the sick young man sitting next to him. "That's him. He's not feeling well. Never found his sea legs."

The customs man turned to the man standing next to him and nodded. Then, he walked off.

The red-haired man, who wore a white shirt, dark trousers and a blue-striped tie and carried a briefcase, sat down across the table from Murphy and Conrad, who hadn't looked up yet. After placing the briefcase on the table, the man extended his right hand to Murphy.

"Hi, I'm Fred Burgess." He wore a concerned expression as he looked toward Conrad. "I'm from the Federated Church of Christ. I work with the war resisters. All the guys call me Reverend Fred."

As they shook hands, Murphy introduced himself. Conrad didn't stir.

Reverend Fred turned his attention to Murphy.

"Are you a friend of his?"

Murphy sat back in his chair. "Not exactly." As he looked toward Conrad, he placed an arm on his shoulder. "We just met. I thought I'd help him out. He's not feeling well."

Burgess unzipped his briefcase, reached inside and removed a few papers. "Did he tell you what he's doing?"

Murphy nodded. "He said he's deserting the army."

Reverend Fred shook his head. "We don't call them deserters. We call them war resisters. They're protesting America's involvement in the Vietnam War."

V.D. would love this guy, Murphy thought, recalling his former partner's disdain for the antiwar movement.

Burgess reached out and touched Conrad on the shoulder.

"Ricky, I need to talk to you before the ship docks," he implored. "We've got to fill out some paperwork before you can enter Sweden."

Conrad stirred. He pushed himself away from the table and sat up in his chair. "Okay," he said, in a soft voice.

Then, Reverend Fred explained the situation.

"Normally, you guys fly into Stockholm, and we meet you at the airport. We have a press conference. And the Swedish government gives its permission for you to stay. But your case is different."

Burgess glanced toward the customs official, who stood watching the card game. "Mr. Johannson has allowed me to come out and escort you."

Reverend Fred picked up one of the sheets of paper and studied it for a moment. "I understand you don't have a passport."

Conrad nodded.

Burgess slid the paper across the table. "You'll have to fill out one of these." Then, the minister removed a ballpoint pen from a holder in the breast pocket of his shirt. He reached over and handed it to Conrad.

Murphy glanced toward the customs man. "That was nice of Mr. Johannson to help you out."

Burgess grinned. "Like Stella Dubois, I often depend upon the kindness of strangers."

"Stella who?"

Reverend Fred chuckled. "Stella. Stella Dubois. She's a character in *A Streetcar Named Desire*, a play by Tennessee Williams."

"Sorry," Murphy said. "I don't go to the theater much."

"Then, I guess we won't be talking much about Pinter or Beckett, will we?" Burgess responded.

The playwrights also were unfamiliar to Murphy. "I guess not."

Murphy glanced toward Conrad, who had picked up the sheet of paper and was reading it. "How did you know our friend was coming? From what he told me, he didn't exactly advertise the fact he was deserting from the Army."

Burgess smiled. "A friend told me," is all he said.

The network Mister Smith talked about, Murphy mused. Again.

Then, it was Reverend Fred's turn to ask questions.

"Why are you going to Sweden, Mr. Murphy?"

Murphy ran a hand through his goatee. "I guess you could say I'm on vacation." Then, he glanced toward the three teen-aged girls. "I am, if you pardon the expression, trying to screw my way through Europe."

Burgess laughed. "A noble enterprise, I'm sure." Then, he glanced toward the three girls. "They're kind of young for you, aren't they?"

Murphy nodded. "You're right," he smiled. "Maybe, I'll find someone my own age in Stockholm."

Next to Murphy, Conrad was busy filling out the form Burgess had given him. He leaned forward, sitting with his left elbow propped on the table, his face buried into his left hand.

"Do you have any questions, Rick?" Burgess asked.

Conrad looked up. "Do I have to give them my father and mother's names and where they live?"

Burgess nodded. "I'm afraid so. You have to list your next of kin."

"Nothing's going to happen to them, right?" Conrad's voice held a note of concern.

Burgess shook his head. "No, Ricky. This is just between you and the United States government. Nothing is going to happen to your family."

Conrad turned the sheet of paper over and began filling out information on the back of it.

Burgess posed another question to Murphy. "How do you feel about what Ricky is doing?"

A good question. Murphy wasn't sure he could answer it honestly.

Murphy shrugged. "I guess it's his business what he does."

Abruptly, Reverend Fred changed his tack. "Were you ever in the military?"

"No." Another lie. But Murphy was emphatic. He had already

decided he wasn't going to admit to any affiliation with the military. "A bum knee kept me out."

The young minister probed a little more.

"What do you think about what we're doing in Vietnam?"

"I try not to think about it." That answer wasn't too far from the truth.

"So, you're a member of the Silent Majority?" A wise crack.

Murphy shook his head. "I really don't belong to anything. I'm not a joiner. Live and let live is what I say."

Murphy didn't like the impression he was making. However, it was much better than telling Burgess he was an Army CID investigator sent to Sweden on an undercover assignment.

Apparently, Reverend Fred had already formed an opinion of Murphy. And it wasn't a flattering one. "I know your type. You just look out for number one."

Another shrug. "What can I say?"

After Conrad finished filling out the immigration form, he slid it back across the table.

Burgess reviewed it. "All the i's are dotted, t's are crossed, I see. We shouldn't have any trouble after we're ashore." He slipped the completed form into his briefcase.

"Mr. Murphy, I want to thank you for helping out Ricky. I appreciate it."

Murphy shrugged. "It was the least I could do."

As he stood up to leave the table, Burgess glanced down at the deck. "Do you have an automobile in the hold?"

Murphy shook his head. "No, I don't."

"Do you need a ride to Stockholm?"

Murphy nodded. "That would be nice."

THAT EVENING, Lund dined at home with his wife.

For dinner, Marta served meatballs, glazed with a tangy chutney sauce, with mixed vegetables and a small bowl of lingonberries on the side. It was one of his favorite dishes.

Lund sat across from his wife at the small trestle table near the large window overlooking the shoreline and the placid waters of Lake Vänern.

Pointing at Lund's dish with her fork, Marta asked: "Is it good?"

Lund nodded, "*Ja.*" Then, he caught himself and translated his thoughts into English. "It is very good. Very spicy."

Marta smiled. "Is it as good as your mother's?"

That was a tough question.

Lund looked down at his plate. He slowly stirred the mixture of meat and vegetables with his fork before he answered. In English. "Oh, it is as good as my mother's, I do believe."

It was a difficult admission. Every boy in Sweden grew up sure his mother made the best meatballs in the country. After all, it was the national dish.

Marta was not done teasing her husband. "Is it better than your mother's?"

This time, Lund paused a little longer as he searched for just the right word. In English. Finally, it came. "Different," he said. "Your meatballs are different."

Lund's wife smiled. "Hmmm. Different is good."

Then, Marta turned serious. "You know, soon I won't be able to cook like this for you." She reached across the table to touch his hand. "School opens next month, and I will become extremely busy again."

Lund took her hand in his. "I know."

Wistfully, Marta glanced out the window. "I love it here at our little cottage at the lake. I wish summer would never end."

Lund raised her hand to his mouth. "Me, too," he murmured before gently brushing the back of her hand with his lips. "I wish summer would never end."

Then, Marta's mood lightened. "Well, summer is not over yet." She treated Lund to a broad smile. "Anita and Peter are coming. And the children. We'll have a good time. We always do."

Unfortunately, Lund couldn't share in her excitement. "Oh, I'm afraid I have some bad news." He looked up to see the smile gone from Marta's pretty face. Lund never liked to be the cause of that. "I don't know how much time I can take off, right now."

His wife sat back in her chair. She gave him an appraising look. "Is it the case? The man in the canal?"

"Yes." Lund shook his head. "I think I will have to move fast on this one."

Very fast, Lund thought.

From the start, Lund had a lot of questions about the case.

Who was the man in the canal?

How did he get there?

Who killed him?

Why was he killed?

And, since talking to Doctor Gustavson that afternoon, perhaps the most important question of all: "What can I do about it?"

Gustavson believed the dead man wasn't Swedish. To make matters worse, evidence—the Globe and Anchor tattoo—indicated the victim might have been an American. If that were true, the NCID would definitely take over the investigation.

A squad of the Boys From Stockholm would descend on Mariestad. Lund would be shunted aside. Oh, he would be given some mundane tasks to do. Maybe, track down a lead or two. But another police inspector would be placed in charge. It wouldn't be his case.

It didn't seem fair. After a long career of conducting humdrum investigations—open-and-shut cases—Lund finally had a real murder case fall into his lap. He didn't want to let it go. He had to find some way to keep it under his control. At least for a while. But how?

Marta wasn't happy with Lund's revelation. "But you and Peter were going to work on the sauna," she reminded him.

Peter had done most of the finish work in the Lunds' remodeled cottage. Every time he came for a visit, he spent some of his time working on a project.

To Peter, building the sauna would be child's play, and Lund was counting on his brother-in-law to help him make short work of it. Within the family it was well known Lund was all thumbs when it came to wielding a hammer or a saw, let alone a soldering iron or a pair of needle nose pliers.

However, Lund was good at doing grunt work. And making plans.

Already that summer, after borrowing a post-hole digger from a farmer friend of his, he had embedded twelve cedar posts more than a meter into the ground on which the platform of the sauna would sit. Also, he'd dug the narrow trench to run the electrical power line to a junction box inside the cottage.

The future sauna was sited next to the cottage toward the lake. The previous owners had planted a row of Norwegian pines as a screen from the other cottages nearby, and it would be built behind that line of evergreens. On the beach side, a small hillock would hide the little building from all but the most discerning boaters on the lake.

Lund's plans called for the construction of a two-by-three-meter wooden structure. Lying under tarpaulin next to the cottage were neat stacks of cedar boards for the flooring, benches and interior walls, two-by-fours for the framing, pine boards for the roof and exterior sheathing, a square of asphalt shingles for the roofing and a couple of cans of red paint that matched the scarlet hue of the cottage.

As usual, Lund was prepared.

However, the murder case meant a change in his plans.

When Peter and his family arrived the next morning Lund would inform him of his dilemma.

Lund knew what his brother-in-law's answer would be.

"No problem."

Then, Lund thought about the favor he intended to ask of his old friend, Doctor Gustavson.

Would the pathologist give him the same answer?

IT WAS still light out when the *Nils Holgersson* docked inside the stone breakwater in the harbor at Trelleborg.

The auto ferry was a bit behind schedule because the pilot had to slowly pick his way around a small fishing boat that had run aground on the shoals near the ships' channel.

Murphy's arrival in Sweden was uneventful. Johansson, the customs agent, took a cursory glance at his passport.

Then, Johansson asked Murphy to empty his pockets. Out came the large wad of money, the box of Rothmans, the Zippo lighter, a black leather wallet containing Murphy's Massachusetts driver's license, the unmarked postcard and four paper clips.

The customs agent picked up the wad of cash like he was gauging its weight. "I guess you have enough to pay for your visit to Sweden."

Johansson then picked up one of the paper clips. "What are these for?"

Murphy shrugged. "They came with the jacket," he wisecracked. "You never know when you might need one."

Johansson, who never bothered to look into the beat-up leather duffel bag slung from Murphy's shoulder, stamped a Swedish entry visa on the back of the page containing stamps from Belgium, the Netherlands and West Germany.

"I see you have been moving around a lot," Johansson said, in his slightly-accented English, handing the passport back to Murphy. "Enjoy your stay in Sweden."

To Conrad, Johansson said nothing.

As they walked to Burgess's car, Murphy glanced back at

the customs agent, who now stood at the front of a long line of passengers carefully scrutinizing the travel documents of each one. "How much did that cost you?"

"Not one krona," Burgess answered. "It's impossible to bribe a Swedish official."

In other parts of the world, Murphy knew that wasn't necessarily the case.

Murphy gestured toward Conrad, who walked behind them like a puppy following his master, seemingly oblivious to his new surroundings. "How come he rates special treatment?"

"Mr. Johansson is a Social Democrat, and he is against the war," Burgess said.

That made no impression on Murphy. "So?"

"In Sweden, political sympathies count for something, Mr. Murphy," Burgess explained. "Johansson supports what the war protesters are doing, and he's willing to help them out."

War protesters? It was the first time Murphy had heard that term used to describe the soldiers who deserted to Sweden to avoid duty in Vietnam.

What would Van Dyck think? Was the old warrant officer rolling over in his grave?

Then Murphy caught himself. That wasn't funny. In the end, he was sure his former partner wasn't enthralled about being in Nam. After all, it killed him.

Murphy glanced back at Conrad. "So, does that help mean bending the rules to let our little friend in?"

Burgess' stride seemed to grow more purposeful, forcing Murphy to pick up the pace. Conrad dawdled behind, apparently unsure whether he wanted to listen to the two older men talk.

The tall, lanky minister got sharp with Murphy. "Mr. Johansson didn't bend any rules." Burgess held up the form the customs official had filled out. "All he did was issue a visitor's visa to

Mr. Conrad. It's standard procedure."

Murphy wondered whether Marlon Andrews, the man he was sent to Sweden to find, had received the same treatment. Did someone like Johansson give him a free pass when he entered the country? Did Fish have to register with the police in Stockholm?

Murphy doubted it. From what Smith said, Andrews was a bad actor. Fish would want stay as far away from government officials as possible. Any official. Any government.

Burgess led them to a little blue Cortina parked on a side street not far from the ferry slip.

"Nice set of wheels," Murphy commented. "If it had wings, I suppose it would fly."

His comment lightened the mood.

"My folks bought it for me in Germany when I came to Sweden," Burgess explained. He popped open the trunk so his two passengers could stow their gear. He sounded apologetic. "Thought it would be good on gas. It's real expensive over here."

When he leaned into the trunk, Murphy noticed the little yellow flower decal pasted to the back of the compact car. "Flower power?" he asked, pointing to the sticker.

"From my little sister." Burgess smiled. "Some radio station up in Maine was giving them away as a promotion when she was going to camp there earlier this summer. I promised her I would put it on my car."

Murphy glanced toward Conrad. "Good to see someone keeps his promises."

If either Burgess or Conrad heard the remark, neither showed it.

However, Murphy nearly bit his tongue. As soon as he made the comment, he wanted to take it back. He had to keep his cool.

As the three men climbed into the car—Murphy in front in the passenger seat next to Burgess and Conrad in the back—the young minister outlined their travel itinerary. "We'll drive to Malmo, where we can gas up and get something to eat. Then, it's an eight or nine-hour drive up to Stockholm." He looked at his watch. "Should get there by four or five o-clock in the morning."

The trip to Trelleborg, a small working seaport that reminded Murphy of the little fishing port of Gloucester in Massachusetts, had already cost Burgess a day. Normally, the young minister had to go no farther than the airport at Arlanda to meet military deserters entering Sweden.

During the short drive to Malmo, Murphy learned why the young minister had to make the trip south to meet Conrad.

"Usually, most war protesters fly into Stockholm," he explained. "However, Mr. Conrad had to take an alternate route."

"I fucked up," Conrad interjected. Almost immediately, the young deserter apologized. "Sorry, Rev. Burgess, I didn't mean to swear."

Burgess laughed. "No need to apologize. You made an accurate assessment. And don't call me Rev. Burgess. Call me Reverend Fred, or just plain Fred, Everyone else does."

From the back seat, Conrad continued his story in his slow drawl, carefully choosing his words as he went along.

"Well, I made a mistake." Then he paused.

"A mistake?" Murphy asked

"Like I told you, after I got my orders, I told my CO I didn't want to go to Vietnam. I asked him to help me get out of it." Another pause.

"I take it he wasn't much help," Murphy offered.

"No, the prick put a watch on me." Conrad looked toward Burgess, momentarily unsure of his choice of words. However, the minister kept his attention on the two-lane road, which followed the coastline west from Trelleborg. "I couldn't get near an airport without someone shadowing me."

Murphy was intrigued. "How did you get to Lubeck? And onto the ferry?"

"A buddy of mine in personnel got me, and my shadow, a five-day leave to Lubeck. We took the train north. No airports. When we got to Travemunde, I bugged out and hopped on the boat."

The network Smith talked about at work again, Murphy assumed.

Burgess then explained the reason for the quick trip to Stockholm. "Before he can be granted the right to stay in Sweden, Mr. Conrad must register with the immigration officials in Stockholm."

No way Marlon Andrews made that trip. Murphy was sure. Fish was too dirty. The Swedes wouldn't let him in as a deserter.

"The Swedish government doesn't grant political asylum to the war protesters," Burgess continued. "However, once they register with the authorities they can stay as long as they like. As long as they follow the rules, they're eligible to receive the benefits every Swedish citizen is entitled to."

Murphy was puzzled. "Rules? Benefits?"

"In order to receive the benefits of Sweden's generous welfare state, the war protesters must learn to speak Svenska," the minister explained. "They must take weekly language lessons. As long as they make an effort to learn the language, they qualify for unemployment and health benefits and educational aid, if they want it."

It was all a revelation to Murphy. He didn't know the deserters had it so good in Sweden. Once they crossed over, he assumed they were on their own, or, at the very least, their families would have to look out for them. To him, it sounded like the military deserters, or protesters as Burgess had referred to them, were treated as heroes by the Swedes. Unemployment benefits? Health benefits? Educational aid? Even the American soldiers returning from Vietnam didn't have it that good.

The whole thing made Murphy sick. It was difficult for him to hide his disgust. With the Swedes. With Burgess. And most of all, with Conrad.

However, the mission demanded Murphy fight off his revulsion. He had to put his personal feelings aside and act like the professional he was.

His assignment required him to maintain his cover. No matter what, Murphy had to pass himself off as a modern-day vagabond, without a care in the world. He mustn't show his antipathy toward the deserters and those people who helped them.

For Murphy, hiding his true feelings could be as difficult as maintaining his cover. He tended to wear his heart on his sleeve. But the situation required him to think a bit more before he spoke. "You gotta look before you leap," Van Dyck often told him. "At least take a peek." As usual, V.D. was right.

Murphy needed to play his role. Stay in character. And, most of all, live in the moment. That was the key. Always.

As Murphy mulled over his situation, he grew quiet. Even in the confines of the small English Ford, he'd become reclusive. During the short drive to Malmo, the large Swedish seaport across the narrow Great Belt strait from Copenhagen, Murphy didn't say another word. He just stared out at the lush pastureland that seemed to run right up to the Baltic Sea.

The stop in Malmo took no more than forty-five minutes. Burgess topped off the Cortina's ten-gallon tank and refilled the small gas can he carried in the trunk. Then, they dined on thick slices of Feta-encrusted pizza at Zorba's, a pizza joint down near the waterfront.

At both stops, Murphy picked up the tab. Each time, he

peeled off about fifty krona from his large wad of bills. No way was he going to freeload on this trip.

During those stops, the conversation had tended toward the mundane. The weather. Pizza. Swedish women. Much of the time, Conrad did most of the talking. He was excited.

"Look at that!" Conrad said. He pointed to a tall blonde girl walking on the sidewalk as Burgess slowly drove the Cortina along a tree-shaded street during the trip across town after they left the docks. "As my pappy would say, that's a tall drink of water."

Keeping in character, Murphy eyed the girl. "Might be a little too young for me," he stated. "But she is a looker."

Burgess was noncommittal.

In order to drive, the tall, lanky minister had to fold legs and arms around the steering wheel like a large, red-headed Praying Mantis. He looked very uncomfortable. Nearly every time he down shifted, he rapped the little knob on top of the gearshift against the side of his leg. However, he eyes never left the road.

Burgess followed the highway northwest along the coast to Helsingborg, where the road turned northeast toward Stockholm.

"Better settle in, boys," Burgess warned as the Cortina rolled through farmland which spread out on both sides of the road. "We got a long drive ahead of us."

At first, Murphy simply watched the countryside roll past. About halfway to Stockholm, the sun finally went down, grudgingly sinking through a purple haze in the western sky. As they drove on in the dark, Murphy picked out the dark outline of a house. Or a barn. Or a silo. Or at least he thought he did.

After a while, Murphy began to think about Kate. He wondered what time it was back in Massachusetts.

What was the time difference? Five, six hours? He looked at

his Seiko. He figured Kate's shift at Mass. General had ended long ago.

Kate worked days. Before heading home to her apartment in Quincy, she'd stop off at her mother's place in Dorchester to pick up Tommy.

Murphy's reverie was broken by something Burgess asked him.

"I didn't catch that," Murphy answered. "What did you say?"

"I said, 'You don't like us very much, do you?' "

"Us?" Murphy glanced into the back seat, where Conrad, curled up into a little ball, had fallen noiselessly asleep.

Burgess went on to explain. "You don't like Mister Conrad for deserting, and you don't like me for helping him. I can tell."

Quite perceptive, Murphy thought.

To Burgess, he said: "Look, I really don't feel one way or the other about you two. Hell, I just met you guys today."

When in doubt, act cavalier. But it didn't work.

Burgess wasn't done. "There was something you said. Back in Trelleborg. After the boat docked. Something about keeping promises."

Apparently, little escapes Reverend Fred, it occurred to Murphy. "I didn't mean anything by that. It just popped into my head and out of my mouth."

That didn't satisfy Burgess. "Well, how do you feel about our sleepy friend back there, and what I'm doing for him?"

A long time ago, Murphy had learned there was nothing wrong about including a kernel of truth when telling a lie. Now was a good time.

"Well, to tell you the truth, I'm not crazy about deserters," Murphy said. That was the truth.

Murphy wasn't done. "My father and all of my uncles fought in World War II, and none of them ever deserted."

Murphy didn't want to debate with the young minister. "Hey man, this war really doesn't concern me." There was a kernel of truth to that statement now.

Looking into the rear-view mirror at the sleeping Conrad, Burgess said, "That's exactly how he feels."

That ended the conversation.

Murphy wanted to tell the young minister more. He wanted to tell him about his own experience in Vietnam. About the small pieces of shrapnel he still carried around in his back. And about the loss of his best friend.

But Murphy knew there was no point in it.

Burgess believed what he believed. And Murphy believed what he believed. A lengthy discussion wouldn't change that.

Besides, Murphy had a cover to maintain.

All he could do was hope the young minister was buying what he was selling.

As the little Cortina scooted through the darkened country-side in the heart of Sweden's lake district Murphy drifted off to sleep.

BEFORE REPORTING for work, Inspector Lund waited for the arrival of Peter and Anita and the children.

The Nillsons lived in the archipelago off Stockholm. Despite leaving their island home well before sunrise to beat the cross-town traffic, it still took them nearly four hours to drive the three hundred kilometers down the E3 to Mariestad.

The ritualistic greetings were followed by the unpacking of Peter's blue-and-white Volvo station wagon. Suitcases and camping gear had been stored in the rooftop carrier, and carpentry tools and a week's worth of groceries had been placed in the rear deck.

Before Lund could take his brother-in-law aside, his niece and nephew, Britta and Arvid, ages eleven and twelve, respectively, had to report their summer adventures to their favorite uncle. Looking tanned and fit, they excitedly told Lund how they soloed their sailboards in the sheltered waters among the islands off Stockholm. Now, they were sure they were ready to crew the little wooden sailing dinghy Lund kept beached in front of the cottage.

"Can we take her out?" Arvid asked.

"Please," Britta implored.

"I'll think about it," was all Lund said.

The small wooden sailboat was not yet seaworthy. It had sat on the sandy beach for most of the summer. Before it could be launched, the little cat-rigged boat needed to be sunk, so the wood could swell up, making its hull watertight. It was something Lund had put off doing. This summer his job and the work on the sauna had left him with little time to sail.

It was after ten o'clock before Lund was able to tell his brother-in-law of his knotty problem.

In general terms, the police inspector told him about the man in the canal.

"I need a few days to devote to the case," he explained. "If I don't move quickly, the boys from Stockholm will move in and take over."

Peter understood.

"No problem," he said.

As expected.

Nilsson reviewed Lund's plans for the sauna.

"Anita can help me with the framing and the exterior sheathing," he said. "The interior will be cramped, so the inside finish work is a one-man job, and I can tie in the electric by myself. Should be a piece of cake."

Lund nodded. "Good." Still, he couldn't help feeling a little guilty about leaving his brother-in-law to fend for himself. "I'll give you a hand when I can."

Peter, a powerfully-built man who stood half-a-head shorter than the tall, slim Lund, patted his brother-in-law on the back. "Don't worry about it. I'll be all right. Just find out who the man in the canal was and then find his killer."

Before Lund left, Peter helped him push the dinghy out into the water. There wasn't a daub of caulking in the small craft's seams. It didn't need it. The little boat would sink in a matter of hours. Maybe, by the next morning, his niece and nephew would be able take it out for its first sail of the summer.

Lund drove the little white Saab to work. Marta wasn't planning on going anywhere anyway. First, she needed to catch up on the family gossip with her sister. Then, she planned to help her niece and nephew erect their large tent among the trees between the cottage and the beach. The youngsters were camping out.

Before going to see Dr. Gustavson, Lund stopped at police headquarters. The Cop Shop. It was quiet. No new information had come in concerning the dead man. The day before, Lund had checked on missing person reports in Stockholm, Gothenburg and Malmo, Sweden's three largest cities. It had now been twenty-four hours since he had filed his request. All of the police agencies had answered his query. None of them had anything to report.

It was a little after noon when Lund finally sat down for his talk with Dr. Gustavson. They met for lunch on the patio of a little bistro on Viktoriagatan, about a kilometer away from the pathologist's lab at the hospital.

"Sorry, I'm late," Lund said. "I had some personal business to attend to. Some visitors, you know."

The doctor nodded. "I understand." Then, Gustavson placed a large manila envelope on the table between them. "I also had a visitor this morning," he started. "A colleague of mine dropped by. He works at the national laboratory. He's down from Stockholm on holiday. Has a place on one of the islands out on the lake. He looked at your waterlogged friend from the canal."

It piqued Lund's interest. "And?"

Gustavson pushed the envelope a little closer to the police inspector. "Open it. Take a look at what's inside."

Carefully, Lund slid the single sheet of paper out of the envelope. It was a composite sketch of a man. A round moon face. Large eyes. Flat nose. Long scraggly hair.

Lund pointed to the mouth of the man in the sketch. "Is your friend sure about this?"

The balding doctor nodded. "Nils is very good at what he does. Even with the bloated condition of the body, he was able to discern it."

Lund gazed at the sketch in wonderment. "A harelip."

Dr. Gustavson beamed. "Exactly."

Using even more care than when he removed it, Lund slid the

composite back into the envelope. "This is a rare occurrence, is it not?"

The doctor nodded again. "Indeed. Between one or two occur per every one thousand births. In a country with a population like Sweden, we would expect to find no more than fifteen thousand people born with some form of this condition. Of course, in a lot of cases, the cleft lip can be surgically repaired. So, in Sweden, that number could be much smaller."

It took the police inspector a few moments to digest this bit of information.

Then, Lund shared his analysis with the doctor. "Of course, since relatively few Americans live in Sweden, the number of men among them with harelips would be much smaller. Is that right?"

Dr. Gustavson agreed. "From an actuarial point of view, that would be true. Among the Americans living in Sweden, very few of them would be expected to share this condition. Statistically-speaking."

Lund smiled. "Then, this sketch should prove extremely helpful in learning the identity of the dead man. It's a distinctive trait, one that is seldom forgotten. Surely, someone somewhere in Sweden will remember an American with a harelip."

The doctor beamed at Lund. "Exactly."

Then, the police inspector's smile faded.

"What's the matter?" Gustavson asked.

"I need to ask a favor."

The doctor made an opened-handed gesture. "What is it?"

Lund looked squarely at Gustavson. "I need some time."

"Go on."

Lund explained his problem as concisely as he could. "I want to work this case, and I'm afraid when NCID learns the body of a murdered American man has been found floating in the Göta

Canal, its investigators will swoop down and take it over. I want a crack at it. For professional reasons."

At first, Gustavson said nothing. Instead, he put his hands together as if he were praying, leaned forward and pinched his pursed lips with his fingertips. Abruptly, he reached for the envelope. "Stockholm doesn't know the cause of death yet," Gustavson pushed the envelope to the police inspector's side of the table.

"I can give you three days. No more. Then I'll have to file the autopsy report."

"Three days?"

"Exactly."

MURPHY AND BURGESS sat in a corner booth sipping glasses of Pripps in the Den Roda Raven.

The small bar was located on Västerlänggatan, one of dozens of narrow cobble-stoned streets crisscrossing Gamla Stan, Stockholm's old town. It was about a block away from the apartment the young minister's church group maintained as a halfway house for military deserters.

They had arrived in Stockholm just as the sun came up, and Burgess took them to the flat. There, Murphy and Conrad camped out on cots in the cramped bedroom, while Burgess dozed on the couch in the tiny living room.

All three of them slept until the middle of the afternoon when two other Americans showed up. The visitors expected to find Conrad in the flat. They were surprised to find Murphy there, too.

"What's your story?" the tallest of two young men asked him.

Murphy put up his hands in mock submission. "I got no story." He gestured toward Conrad. "I'm not with him. I'm just passing through."

Burgess interceded. "Mr. Murphy, as he so charmingly puts it, is screwing his way through Europe." He smiled. "He's all right."

Apparently, the tall, lanky minister's stamp of approval was enough. Anyway, it was clear the men weren't interested in Murphy. At least not now. Quickly, their attention turned to Conrad, the one they'd really come to see.

"We need some time alone with him, Reverend Fred," Murphy's questioner said. "Is it okay if we use your place?"

Murphy and Burgess were banished to the Den, as Americans who lived in the neighborhood called the pub, to nurse

glasses of weak Swedish beer and listen to the music of Cre-
dence Clearwater Revival blaring in the background.

"Tastes a lot like water," Murphy commented following his first
sip of the draft beer.

"It's three point two beer," Burgess explained. "Until recently,
it was the only type of beer brewed in Sweden."

The Den Roda Raven reminded Murphy of the little neighborhood bars back in Southie. The old wooden-boothed estab-
lishments, which had sprung up throughout The Hub before
World War II following the repeal of prohibition, never seemed
to change. His uncles bought Murphy his first beer long before
it was legal for him to drink in Massachusetts, in a bar like The
Den in Dorchester. It was a frosty glass of Narragansett, or
"Nastygansett" as one uncle called it, and Murphy remembered
how he didn't like its bitter lager taste. His glass of Pripps didn't
taste bitter, just watery.

The Den's walls were adorned with pictures of its namesake.
Large blown-up photographs of red foxes, Sweden's most abun-
dant wild animal, were prominently displayed on its walls. A fox
sitting in a grassy glade. Another fox, its long tale trailing behind
it, running through a grove of trees. A fox lying with her kits in a
den. Everywhere Murphy looked, a picture of a fox or a group
of foxes hung on the wall. Foxes. Lots of them. In every setting
imaginable.

Not long after they sat down, they learned they had common
roots.

The young minister grew up in western Massachusetts in In-
terlacken, a village tucked in the woody hollows between the
small towns of Lenox and Stockbridge, across the state from
Cape Cod, where Murphy grew up.

Growing up in the Commonwealth of Massachusetts they
found was the only thing the two men had in common.

In high school, Murphy played sports. Football. Basketball. Baseball. A little golf while he worked at the old course in Harwich.

The tall, gangly Burgess admitted he had absolutely no athletic ability. In high school, he was a bookworm.

Following his graduation, Burgess, who was two or three years younger than Murphy, went to Yale, where he got involved in the burgeoning anti-war movement. Then, he spent two more years at Andover Newton in Massachusetts obtaining his Master of Divinity.

Murphy didn't tell Burgess he joined the army right after high school. Instead, he told him how he worked as a stern man on a lobster boat.

Like most of the lies Murphy concocted while working undercover, it contained a grain of truth. One summer while he was high school, he did work out of Falmouth on a lobster boat. He embellished his experience.

Murphy told Burgess how he'd hurt his knee while pulling traps off Nantucket. "Reached for a high flyer on a string of traps and nearly fell out of the boat," he said. "The sea was running rough and I banged up my knee real bad climbing back in." The injury left him with a 4-F draft status and kept him out of the service, Murphy claimed.

However, Murphy didn't stop there.

"Since then, I sort of bummed around," he said. It sounded plausible. "Working odd jobs. Spent a lot of time working in bars on the Jersey shore. Atlantic City. At a place in Manasquan that claimed to have the longest bar in the world. Wildwood."

Not everything Murphy told Burgess about his work life was a total fabrication.

After returning from duty in Vietnam more than three years before, Murphy served a stint at Fort Dix, the sprawling U.S.

Army base in south New Jersey's pine barrens. On various undercover assignments, he'd worked in bars up and down the Jersey shore. He knew just enough about those places to make his story sound convincing.

As Van Dyck, his former partner, used to tell Murphy, every good lie has to have a bit of truth in it. Over the years, during one undercover assignment after another, Murphy, with his poker face and intense manner, had become a master at it.

From what Burgess said about his background, Murphy doubted the young minister had much experience in the world he inhabited. He probably didn't possess the knowledge to poke holes in the yarn Murphy had spun.

Besides, after the conversation started, the young minister was more interested in talking about himself, anyway. Murphy let him have the floor.

Not long after Murphy and Burgess had taken up residence in their corner booth, a man came into the pub and sat on a stool at one end of bar across the room. Something about him, and the way he acted, caught Murphy's attention. As Burgess talked, Murphy kept an eye on him.

While Burgess explained how he became a man of the cloth, the little man at the bar left his stool to follow one of the bar's other patrons into the bathroom. It was the second time it happened since Murphy began watching him. He'd seen that move before.

Burgess said his interest in the ministry began as a young boy. He talked about the special sermons the minister used to deliver to the children in the front pews of the old Congregational church in Stockbridge. "He was such a nice fellow, warm and friendly," the young minister recalled. "He always had props he would use to illustrate his sermon. Hand puppets. Things like that. Sometimes, he would give us candy."

As Murphy listened to Burgess, he noticed how the man at the bar came out of the bathroom less than thirty seconds after he went in. As he climbed back on his stool, he shoved something into the pocket of his old army field jacket. Murphy knew what was up.

During several undercover assignments, Murphy had often tailed drug dealers around Philadelphia and in New York City while they made their drops. Those guys were much smoother than this fellow. They were more discreet. In a public place, such as a bar like the Den, they usually handed off what they were peddling and collected the money in separate operations through a number of relays. That way, they seldom got caught holding the drugs and the money at the same time.

This dealer, a short, wiry man who slicked his dark hair straight back from his face, didn't use a cutout. To Murphy, it looked as if this fellow carried the drugs in one pocket and the money in another. Not too bright.

As Murphy watched another deal go down at the other end of the pub, Burgess told him about Mr. Brown and the bell tower at his church in Stockbridge.

"Every day at five-thirty, he'd ring the chimes for a half hour," Burgess explained. "Sometimes, he let us kids help. I've never forgotten how religious he was in his duty. It's always stayed with me."

This time, a young, thin woman sat down on the stool next to the drug dealer. The barman, a big, burly fellow, took her order and moved down to the taps at the other end of the bar to draw a glass of beer. The woman placed something on the bar. The drug dealer removed a small packet from the pocket of his field jacket and placed it on the counter. Then, before the barman returned with the beer, the man and the woman picked up what each had left for the other on the bar top. The transaction took just a few moments.

While Burgess droned on about Mr. Brown and the chimes, Murphy decided he'd seen enough. He needed to know more about the man at the bar.

"Hate to change the subject, Reverend Fred, but do you know who that guy is sitting at the end of the bar? The one with the glass of beer in his hand," Murphy gestured toward the compactly-built young man with the slicked-back hair.

"Which fellow?" Burgess asked. He shifted slightly in his seat to eye the bar. "Oh, him." Burgess returned his gaze to Murphy. "That's Mouse."

"Mouse?" Murphy, who didn't have to change position in his seat to watch the other side of the pub, took another long look. He studied the features of the little man at the end of the bar. In a few moments, he returned his gaze to Burgess. "I see what you mean."

In profile, with his thin, pointed nose, receding chin and hair swept back into a slick little tail, the drug dealer did look like a little rodent.

"Is he Swedish?"

"No. He's an American."

Again, Murphy noticed the old Army field jacket Mouse wore. "Is he one of the deserters, I mean, war protesters?"

Burgess chuckled. "No. Not even close. I doubt he's ever been in the service. He probably did come over to avoid the draft. But he isn't one of my guys."

Murphy gazed at Mouse, who appeared unaware of the attention he had drawn from the two men in the booth at the other end of the pub.

"What's he do?" The answer was obvious, but Murphy wanted to hear what the young minister had to say.

Burgess kept his eyes focused on Murphy. "He just hangs around. About every two, three weeks he shows up. Always seems to have plenty of money. But he has no visible means of support. Most of my guys avoid him."

"My guys?" Murphy commented. It was the second time Burgess had said that.

The minister smiled. "Excuse the expression. But I guess I have a proprietary interest in them. I care what happens to them."

After looking at his watch, Murphy changed the subject again. "Those boys have been talking to young Mr. Conrad for quite a while. Must be giving him the third degree."

Burgess grew serious. "They want to make sure he is who he says he is."

"Why is that so important?"

The young minister leaned forward to make sure only Murphy heard what he was saying. "A lot of the war protesters are concerned about their group being infiltrated by American agents."

"Sounds a bit paranoid," Murphy commented.

"It's a reasonable concern," Burgess said. "Just before I got here last year, a couple of agents from the Army CID encouraged one of the guys to go back. They told him nothing would happen to him. He was real homesick, so he went back."

"So?" Murphy interjected.

"After he got back to Germany, the Army threw the book at him. Sentenced him to hard time. Since then, a lot of the war protesters have become very leery about who they talk to. And they're very concerned about who joins their ranks. They don't want the U.S. military sending people up here from Germany to keep tabs on them."

For a moment, Murphy wondered about his own status. What would the two men who were grilling Conrad say if they knew he was an Army CID investigator in Sweden looking for a killer among them?

"Surely, the Swedish government must keep an eye on all

these guys," Murphy said.

"Not as much as you'd think." Burgess leaned back on his bench. "After they're registered with the government and begin attending language classes, they are free to live anywhere in the country."

That was news to Murphy. "You mean, the deserters are not all here in Stockholm?"

Burgess nodded. "To be sure, a large number of the war protesters live in Stockholm. However, the majority of them are dispersed throughout Sweden. It's not easy to keep up with them."

When Mr. Smith briefed Murphy in Lubeck about his assignment, he didn't mention a word about that. For the first time, he realized Marlon Andrews, the man he was after, could be holed up anywhere in Sweden.

"Most of these guys just want to be left alone," Burgess continued. "Oh sure, some of them are involved in the anti-war movement here. They organize. Take part in peace demonstrations. But most are simply starting new lives here. They have jobs. Some are going to college. Some have gotten married."

Jobs. College. Marriage. That doesn't sound like Fish, thought Murphy. Andrews isn't interested in starting over. He just doesn't want to get caught.

"Not all of the, ah, war protesters are good citizens, are they?" Murphy asked.

"No, not all of these guys are model citizens," Burgess frowned. "A few of them are in prison. A bad apple is a bad apple, no matter which basket it's in."

Murphy gazed at Mouse, who sat at the bar bobbing his head in rhythm to CCR's "Looking Out My Back Door."

Whose basket was that bad apple in?

Murphy wasn't interested in any of the military deserters.

It was different with Mouse.

AFTER HIS VISIT with Doctor Gustavson, Lund went to the police department's new offices on Marieholmsbron to await Officer Gunderson's return from afternoon patrol.

While he waited, the police inspector formulated a plan of action.

First, Lund decided to distribute flyers featuring the composite drawing of the dead man in the canal to police stations throughout Sweden. Maybe the murder victim was known to the police in Stockholm, Malmo, or Gothenburg or Jonkoping. It was routine. Information about missing persons often was sent out in this fashion.

Next, Lund needed to take a trip to Stockholm to visit the immigration board. Maybe, an American émigré with a harelip would raise a red flag for one of the officials in that department. Maybe, it would provide a lead for him to narrow the focus in his search for the dead man's identity.

Finally, Lund needed to enlist the aid of Officer Gunderson. The investigation would require some legwork. Due to Dr. Gustavson's deadline, time was of the essence. Maybe, the young policeman wouldn't mind passing up his patrol duties for a few days to help the police inspector do some real police work.

Primarily, Lund wanted Gunderson's help because the young man owned a car, a two-year-old Audi he picked up for a song during one of his forays into West Germany to play ice hockey. After women, Swedish females of every shape and size, hockey seemed to be the young policeman's greatest passion.

During his trip to Stockholm, Lund wanted to maintain a low profile. No sense driving around in a blue and white, with the words "*Polisen*" painted prominently on its side.

Lund couldn't take the Saab because his wife might need it. The Nillsons had a car. But the police inspector didn't want to impose on them any more than he had. Already he had abandoned his brother-in-law and stuck him with the construction of the sauna. Of course, Peter didn't mind. To him, the sauna was a labor of love. But it didn't seem right to take the Saab away from Marta and, should the need arise, force her to borrow the Nillson's station wagon.

No. During Lund's investigation, Gunderson would provide the transportation. And backup. The inspector had no idea what he was getting into. It was best to have some support.

Although he would never tell him, Lund enjoyed the company of Gunderson, who had been assigned to Mariestad after joining the Swedish Police Service nearly three years before. To the veteran police inspector, the younger man's brashness and confident manner were endearing qualities; a counterweight to Lund's reserved, nearly stoic, manner.

Lund seldom tooted his own horn. By contrast, Gunderson often sounded like an entire brass section. When the Swedish police were nationalized six years before, Lund's reluctance to brag about his accomplishments probably cost him an assignment with the National Criminal Investigation Department in Stockholm. Under the new setup, Gunderson's personality would result in his rapid advancement, Lund was convinced.

Not that Gunderson was overly ambitious. He did have good work habits, and he looked good in his uniform. However, at this stage of his life, Gunderson, who wore his hair in a long modish style, was more interested in playing hockey and chasing women, not necessarily in that order, than in doing police work.

While growing up in Stockholm, Gunderson dreamed of playing professional ice hockey, maybe becoming the first Swede since Ulf Sterner to play in the National Hockey League in North

America. However, a broken ankle ended that. Gunderson, a strapping six-foot-two, two-hundred-ten-pound defenseman, still played the game, but at nowhere near the skill required to play in the Elitserian, Sweden's top professional league, let alone the NHL.

It took Lund about an hour to put the flyer together. In his prototype, he pasted a reduced version of the composite drawing Dr. Gustavson provided him in the center of a large sheet of white paper.

Above the picture, in English, Lund posed the question: "Do You Know This Man?" in large type. Underneath the query, in smaller print, was a copy block containing a brief physical description of the dead man, the circumstances surrounding the discovery of his corpse, and Lund's contact information.

Below the picture, the same headline and copy block was printed in Svenska.

No mention was made of the Globe and Anchor tattoo. At this point, Lund saw no reason to tell every policeman in Sweden he probably had a dead American on his hands. He wanted that nugget to become public later rather than sooner.

When he was done, the police inspector admired his work. Simple but effective.

After receiving directions on the use of the department's new telephone facsimile machine from the dispatcher, who was interrupted twice during her dissertation by incoming calls, the police inspector began transmitting the document to other police stations.

It was a slow, laborious process.

The American-made device was state of the art. However, it still took about six minutes for each transmission. After each transmittal, the document had to be removed from the device's metal cylinder then reloaded before Lund could dial the telephone number of the receiving machine at another police station. While the flyer was transmitted to police stations throughout Sweden, Lund kept busy. In between his sessions with the facsimile machine, he caught up on paperwork. Routine stuff. All of it could have waited for a few days. But Lund wanted to keep his new desk clear.

In addition, the police inspector placed two telephone calls.

During a phone call to Stockholm, Lund set up an appointment with an S. Waldman, an official at the immigration board for the following day. "I don't know if we can be of much help," said the woman who set up the meeting. "There are a lot of Americans in Sweden, and it is not easy to keep track of them all."

During the other call to the mental-health facility down near Helsingborg, Lund learned the arsonist he took into custody the previous day was not doing well. Apparently, Into Soumi had arrived at the destination in a near-catatonic state. He'd been placed on suicide watch. "No sharp objects," an attendant at the facility told Lund. "We even took away his shoe laces. We check on him every hour."

After making the call, the police inspector wondered if he'd been wrong to arrest the man and send him away. Second-guessing was a practice Lund tried to avoid. It was a bad habit.

By the time Gunderson returned from his patrol, Lund had wrapped up his paperwork. He was ready to talk about the case. It took him only a few moments to bring the young policeman up to speed.

"Interesting, Max," Gunderson commented, after he read Lund's report and looked at the composite drawing of the dead man. "Looks like you have a murder on your hands."

Lund corrected him. "It looks like we have a murder on our hands."

Gunderson took another look at the composite. "We?"

The police inspector nodded. "Yes, we. I need your help, Ulf."

Gunderson chuckled. "I'm no detective. I'm just a dumb cop."

Picking up his police report from the desk, Lund informed the young policeman of the deadline he faced.

"I've got just three days to wrap this up before Dr. Gustavson passes his findings on to the boys in Stockholm," he explained. "When they learn the victim was American, they'll rush in and take over. I don't want that to happen." The police inspector put his report into the top drawer of his desk. "There's a lot of work to do, and I can't do it by myself."

Lund showed the flyer he'd made to Gunderson. "I sent this to police departments throughout the country. Hopefully it will bear fruit. We may have some leads to follow."

Then the inspector told the young policeman about the appointment he'd scheduled for the following morning with the official at the immigration board. "Even with the scant information we have about the victim—the Globe and Anchor tattoo, the harelip—they might be able to point us in the right direction," he said. "It's a start."

After listening to Lund's plans, Gunderson sounded enthusiastic. "When do we start?" He wore a big grin.

The police inspector hovered over his desk putting copies of the flyer into his briefcase. "We must drive up to Stockholm first thing in the morning."

Gunderson wore an expectant grin. "Can I take The Rocket?"

"No," Lund answered. "The Dodge stays here."

The police inspector's expression returned to its normal grimness as he delivered his marching orders to the young policeman.

"I want to keep this low key," Lund explained. "We'll take your car."

Then, almost as an afterthought, the police inspector added: "Save your receipts for gasoline, and I'll see you are reimbursed. And Ulf, another thing, wear civilian clothes. A tie and a jacket. But bring your service pistol and your badge."

Even though he'd been denied another opportunity to drive the department's powerful Dodge Polara to Stockholm, Gunderson seemed happy about the assignment.

"I get to act like a real detective," the young policeman observed. "That should be fun."

"I hope so." Lund closed the clasp on his briefcase. "Now, you go get ready, and I'll see you in the morning. Say, about seven?"

Gunderson turned to leave.

"Oh, Ulf, there's one more thing."

Another afterthought.

Gunderson stopped at the door.

"When you pick me up tomorrow morning, bring your swim trunks."

Gunderson's expression turned quizzical. "Swim trunks?"

Lund nodded. "That's right."

MURPHY SAT with Reverend Fred for nearly two hours at The Den sipping beer waiting for Conrad to join them.

Murphy was a good listener. It was a strong suit of his.

Burgess had done most of the talking.

While they waited for Conrad, Murphy saw four more drug deals go down. Each one followed a similar pattern. The customer would come into the bar. If it was a male, Mouse followed him into the small restroom off the end of the bar. If it was a female, she sat down on the stool next to him.

Murphy noticed something else.

Nothing happened while the bartender, who seldom smiled as he went about his business, was nearby.

All of the transactions took place while the barman was elsewhere, taking orders from the few customers who sat in the booths and filling them from the three beer taps at the far end of the bar, away from Mouse. No waitress was on duty, so the barman kept moving around. Murphy doubted he even knew what the little man who sat at the end of the bar was up to.

Finally, Conrad showed up. He wore a relieved expression. Apparently, the young deserter had passed muster.

"Are they going to let you join their club?" Murphy asked, as Conrad sat down next to Burgess on the other side of the table.

Conrad nodded. "I'm not supposed to talk about it."

"Oh, I see," Murphy grinned. "You learned the secret handshake and everything."

No one else laughed.

Looking at his watch, Burgess nudged Conrad. "It's getting late. We've got to get going." Reverend Fred gave the young deserter a gentle shove as he slid along the wooden bench the two men shared. "We still have time to go to the immigration board and sign you in. You've got a lot of paperwork to fill out."

After the two men climbed out of their side of the booth, Burgess looked down at Murphy. "You coming?"

A few moments earlier, two pretty blondes had entered The Den and sat down in a booth in the opposite corner of the bar.

"I don't think so." Holding an empty beer glass in his hand, Murphy gestured toward the two women. "I'm going to make like a Polaroid. I'm going to stick around and see what develops."

Before he left, Burgess reached for his wallet. But Murphy stopped him. "Don't worry about it, Rev. I'll pick up this one. It's on me."

"Everything seems to have been on you, lately," the young minister commented. "Thanks."

After Burgess and Conrad left, Murphy ordered another beer. He handed twenty krona to the bartender when he brought the glass back the table. As the barman reached into a pouch in the front of his apron to make change, Murphy put up his hands. "Keep it. It's yours."

"*Tach sa mycket*," A hint of a smile played at the corner of the barman's thick lips. Then he mouthed, a heavily-accented "thank you" and trod back behind the bar.

The two young women who sat in the booth not far from Murphy were very attractive. However, his attention was focused elsewhere. On Mouse.

Besides, Murphy just wasn't interested. Van Dyck must be rolling over in his grave, he thought. The old warrant officer always was interested. "Nothing wrong with getting something a little strange," his former partner often told him.

That no longer worked for Murphy. Hopefully, Kate was still waiting for him back home. Hopefully, he could patch things up with her. Murphy was sure she was all he needed.

He didn't need anything strange. Anymore.

By the time Mouse left his perch at the end of the bar, Murphy had sipped half of his beer. He waited until after the little drug dealer walked out the front door before leaving his booth.

Murphy didn't think it would be difficult to follow the little man with the greased-back hair. But tailing Mouse through Gamla Stan without being noticed proved to be a challenge.

Located on an island in the heart of Stockholm, Gamla Stan wasn't large, a little more than a kilometer wide. But it was honeycombed with narrow cobbled-stoned streets and alleys, and most of them were closed to automobiles. As he trailed the little drug dealer, there was nowhere for Murphy to hide.

After their arrival earlier that day, Burgess parked his Cortina in a dead-end alley down off Skeppbrokajen near the waterfront. Before the young minister could back in, Murphy and Conrad had to get out of the car. Reverend Fred parked with the passenger side of the compact snug against one side of the narrow passageway so he could open his door to get out of the car on the driver's side.

For five minutes, Murphy followed Mouse on a walk up and down several narrow streets. Hanging back, he watched as the little drug dealer sauntered along like he didn't have a care in the world.

Along the way, Murphy noted his surroundings.

Gamla Stan was a slum. The stone facing on most of its buildings was faded and stained. The wooden frames around doors and windows cried out for a coat of paint. It appeared the landlords of the three and four-story apartment houses had simply given up on their upkeep.

As he trailed Mouse, Murphy detected odors. The unmistakable tang of marijuana permeated the air on one street. In another alley, the smell of overcooked turnips nearly overwhelmed him.

The streets were so narrow in this part of Gamla Stan, Murphy doubted much sunlight ever reached the lowest parts of some of the buildings. After it rained, those portions of the old structures probably never dried out. Maybe, that musty dampness was what Murphy smelled the most.

If Mouse knew he was being followed, he didn't let on.

Murphy kept some distance between them. Probably, the little drug dealer didn't even know he was there.

Murphy had plenty of practice. One summer, while working undercover out of Fort Dix, he tailed off-duty soldiers while they made drug buys in Philadelphia and in Brooklyn. None of them knew he was there. Not until he testified against them at their court martial. Only then did they finally notice him. Murphy knew what he was doing.

The end of the trail came when Mouse turned up a narrow passageway—less than two meters wide—on a steep incline.

As Mouse went up the stone steps, Murphy waited at the bottom sneaking peeks around the corner. About halfway up the alley, Mouse stopped. He entered one of the attached houses.

While he waited for Mouse to reappear, Murphy tried to grab a smoke. But his Zippo didn't work. Not enough spark. He dropped the cigarette on the ground. He'd been trying to quit anyway.

While Murphy waited at the corner there was very little traffic up or down the narrow passageway. The few times he did hear someone scuffling along the stairway, Murphy took a quick look around the corner. No Mouse.

During one of those furtive glances, Murphy did notice a man standing at the top of the passageway, a little more than fifty yards away. A few moments later, he took another look. The man seemed to be doing the same thing Murphy was doing. Waiting.

The man who stood at the top of the passageway wore the

same scruffy-looking clothes as nearly every other man Murphy had seen in Gamla Stan, an old Army field jacket and jeans. It must be the uniform of the day, Murphy thought.

However, there was something different about this man. He looked healthy. Indeed, he appeared more physically fit than any of the hippie-types Murphy had observed during his meandering around the neighborhood.

Murphy's former partner, Van Dyck, had always told him: "It takes one to know one." This was one time Murphy agreed with that notion. He was sure the man at the top of the passageway was a cop. Like him, he was waiting for someone. And Murphy was sure that someone was Mouse.

Fifteen minutes after going into the apartment house, Mouse reappeared. Immediately, he started walking down the stone steps in Murphy's direction.

Murphy made a split-second decision.

As Mouse walked his way, Murphy turned the corner and began walking up the passageway toward him. Silently, he glided by the little drug dealer as they passed each other. Murphy kept walking. By the time he'd gotten past the wooden door Mouse had entered, the man who had been standing at the top of the passageway also had walked past him, following Mouse down the steep set of stone steps. He was slightly taller than Murphy, with dark modishly cut hair and a day-old growth on his face.

Close up, he bore a strong resemblance to Tonto, the Lone Ranger's faithful Indian companion. He was slimmer and lighter-skinned, but he wore the same intense expression as the Indian sidekick. He seemed too focused on his quarry to even notice Murphy. He bore down the stairway after Mouse.

Definitely a man on a mission, it occurred to Murphy. Another cop.

Murphy dropped off Mouse's trail. At least, for now. Instead, the CID investigator wanted to know why the little drug dealer had spent so much time in the nondescript house in this narrow alley in Gamla Stan. Most of the drug deals Murphy had witnessed had taken just seconds to go down. But Mouse had spent a considerable amount of time here. Why?

After climbing all the way to the top of the passageway, Murphy checked to see whether Mouse and the man who was tailing him had turned the corner at the bottom. When he was sure the two men had left, Murphy walked back down. Stopping in front of the door, which had a faded number six on it, he looked up and down the steep passageway before entering the building.

He saw no one.

However, before Murphy reached for the door knob, the door swung open, and a man walked through the doorway, nearly knocking him over.

"*Ursahta mig,*" the man said after the slight collision.

"What?"

The man switched to English. "Oh, excuse me," he intoned. A slightly built, olive-skinned man who stood nearly a head shorter than Murphy, he spoke with a different accent than the Swedes Murphy had come in contact with.

"No problem," Murphy answered.

"You looking for Mouse?" the man volunteered. From his accent, and his appearance, Murphy guessed he was from the Middle East. Maybe Turkey.

Murphy nodded.

"Back there." The man jerked his thumb back over his shoulder.

Following the gesture, Murphy noticed a door at the far end of the narrow, dimly-lit hallway. A few steps inside the doorway, a steep staircase led to the upper stories of the narrow apartment house.

Apparently, Mouse's neighbors knew what he was into. Whatever it was didn't seem to bother them.

The building faced west, and, as a result of the late afternoon sun, a narrow shaft of light angled down the hallway from a small window on the second floor of the open vestibule. After walking to the door at the end of the hallway, Murphy noticed the shiny new Yale lock, spotlighted by the narrow beam of light.

For a moment, Murphy checked himself. What would Van Dyck do?

For one thing, the old warrant officer wouldn't be working alone.

He'd have someone watching his back. The one time Murphy's former partner didn't have a backup, it cost him dearly. He paid for it with his life.

But it was different with Murphy. During the past four years, he had become accustomed to working alone. With no safety net. He tried to be cautious, but he wasn't afraid to take some risks.

Turning slightly, Murphy looked back down the hallway. It still was empty, and the front door was closed.

Then, he jammed his right hand into his jacket pocket and felt around for a second. When he removed it, he held one of his paper clips between his thumb and forefinger.

Next, Murphy twisted the paper clip until it snapped in two. Then he bent each piece into a small L-shaped tool.

While standing off to one side so the lock remained in the shaft of light, Murphy worked one of the fabricated lock picks into the keyhole, ramming it in until he was sure all the tumblers were locked in place.

Finally, Murphy slid the other pick inside the keyhole and deftly sprung the lock. He pulled down on the padlock, and the shackle sprung open. A simple twist removed the lock from the hasp.

The whole operation took thirty seconds.

It was a skill Murphy had picked up early in his Army career while stationed with a military police unit in the Philippines. Sometimes, MPs used the technique to open footlockers during surprise barracks inspections. Murphy had become quite adept at springing padlocks open.

Murphy slipped the lock into his jacket pocket.

Before stepping inside the open door, Murphy checked the hallway one last time. Nothing. He stepped in and closed the door behind him.

The room was empty. Even in the dim light, Murphy could see a naked light bulb in the fixture that dangled from the low ceiling. He reached up and screwed in the light bulb to light up the room.

It took Murphy only a few moments to inventory the contents of the small room. He stood next to a twin-sized bed. A small, wooden armoire sat diagonally across the room from the door. A dry sink with a large white ceramic ewer decorated with blue flowers and matching water pitcher stood in the corner opposite the door.

The furnishings were bare bones. Nothing fancy. The room was a place for someone who was just passing through to hang his hat for a few days. From what little Murphy already knew of him, the room would fit Mouse's purposes.

Murphy moved quickly. Inside the armoire, he found a backpack. In its main compartment, he discovered a couple of changes of clothes and some dirty underwear. No drugs.

Inside one of the backpack's zippered compartments, Murphy found toiletries. A razor. A can of shaving cream. A small green bottle of Brut. A toothbrush and a rolled-up tube of Colgate. But no drugs.

As he looked through Mouse's possessions, Murphy remembered the last time he and Van Dyck had conducted a search together. He recalled how they looked through the personal effects of a dead man in a barracks at Phu Bai in South Vietnam more than four years before. A long time ago.

Suddenly, those thoughts were interrupted by footsteps.

Soundlessly, moving like a big cat, Murphy quickly stepped to the door. Putting an ear against it, he listened. For a moment, all he heard was the steady thump-thump of his heartbeat. Then, a floorboard creaked as someone slowly climbed the stairs.

That sound was a reminder. It told Murphy this was no time to think about the past. He had to focus on the present. The past had to stay where it belonged. He had to live in the moment.

After putting all of the items he had discovered back into the backpack where he had found them, Murphy resumed his search.

He looked under the bed.

Nothing.

He rolled back the mattress to reveal a thin layer of metal springs.

Again nothing.

With his hand, Murphy felt along the underside of the dry sink.

More nothing.

Then, Murphy got down on his hands and knees again. He checked the underside of the armoire, which stood no more than a foot off the floor.

Bingo!

Taped to the bottom of the freestanding closet was a rolled-up paper bag. Gingerly, Murphy removed the sack from its hiding place. Careful not to pull the thick masking tape off the bag, he unrolled it and dumped its contents onto the bed.

Inside the bag was the mother lode. A half-dozen dime bags of marijuana. A ball of aluminum foil containing about five grams of hashish. A narrow strip of paper punctuated with twenty to thirty dark little dots, hits of LSD. A small brown pill bottle containing nearly ten tablets of Speed. A matchbook, with a red, white and green replica of the Italian flag on its cover. And a wad of money—mostly Swedish krona—held together by a rubber band.

As Murphy surveyed the stash of drugs laying on the bed, it occurred to him that Mouse was not as dumb as he looked.

During his meanderings around Gamla Stan, the little drug dealer carried just enough dope to make five or six small transactions. If the Swedish police picked him up, he could argue he was a user and not a pusher. Maybe, they'd let him off.

Then, Murphy thought about Tonto, the intense-looking man he'd observed tailing Mouse. Obviously, the Swedish police were on to him.

Why didn't they move in?

Murphy thought about it.

Maybe, the Swedes were looking for someone else. Murphy looked down at the drugs. This was small potatoes. Not much of an operation. Maybe, the Swedish police were looking for a bigger fish.

Maybe, like Murphy, they were looking for Marlon Andrews.

Just then, another sound came from the hallway.

More footsteps.

It took Murphy three long strides to move across the room. As he leaned his shoulder into the door, he heard a whisper come from the other side of it: "*Mus? Mus?*" Those two words were followed by a short string of more Swedish words.

The soft voice definitely belonged to a woman. Perhaps she was one of Mouse's customers. Maybe even a girlfriend.

Murphy was tempted to open the door a crack to take a peek. But he resisted. Instead he stayed in place and leaned his full weight against the door.

"*Mus? Mus?*" This time, it was more of an entreaty. A plea. Again, the words were followed by a string of Svenska.

Whoever it was wanted to see Mouse real bad.

Murphy tensed up.

From the other side of door came more Swedish words. But the woman's tone was different. She sounded puzzled. Then, she grew silent.

That silence was followed by footsteps retreating down the hallway, then the sound of the front door closing as the unexpected visitor left the building.

Murphy relaxed.

But not for long.

At least the Swedish woman hadn't seen him. But she might mention the unlocked door the next time she saw Mouse, and that could be enough to rattle him.

It was clear Murphy had to vacate the premises. Now. He moved quickly, making sure everything in the room was as he'd found it. He didn't want to leave any evidence of his visit. He didn't want to give Mouse cause for concern.

Before Murphy put the drugs back into the hiding place, he checked the paper bag once more. This time he came up with something else—another matchbook.

Murphy thought about his Zippo. He thought about how much he wanted a cigarette. He nearly slipped one of the matchbooks into the pocket of his field jacket. He resisted the urge. Even Mouse might miss a book of matches,

Murphy returned the stash of drugs to exactly where Mouse had hidden them under the armoire. Carefully, he pressed the strips of masking tape into their original crisscross pattern. He hoped the laws of gravity wouldn't undue his work.

Before unscrewing the light bulb, Murphy slowly surveyed Mouse's room one more time—a final check.

When Murphy was sure everything was as it had been when he entered, he left the room, locking the door behind him.

INSPECTOR LUND returned to his home on the shore of Lake Vänern in time for dinner.

For their first meal with the Nillsons, Marta outdid herself. She served a wide variety of pickled herring fillets, bread, cheese and boiled new potatoes she purchased during an afternoon trip with Anita into Mariestad. During the meal, Lund split a bottle of schnapps with Peter.

Right after dinner, at the behest of Arvid and Britta, Lund checked on the dinghy's status. The boat sat in a meter of water no more than ten meters from the shore, a little wooden reef on the sandy lake bottom.

Of the two children, Arvid was the more impatient. "Is it ready, Uncle Magnus? Can we take it out of the water? Will it float?"

Britta, the younger of the two siblings, stood silently next to her uncle on the beach, in total awe of him as usual.

Lund knew the boat needed to remain submerged for close to twenty-four hours before the thin sheets of marine plywood which made up its hull would swell enough to close the seams. He was proud he had never used a bead of caulking to make the little boat watertight. Once its dunking was complete, and nature took its course, the dinghy would bob in the water like a little cork. One night in the water should do it.

"Tomorrow morning, we'll have some help, and we'll take the boat out of the water and float it," Lund promised the children.

That announcement seemed to satisfy Lund's niece and nephew. They discussed their plans to sail on the lake the next day.

"Just in sight of camp," Anita, their mother, reminded them. "You sail just in sight of the cottage or you sail no more."

"Yes, mama," Arvid and Britta chorused. "We sail just in sight of the cottage."

Lund reviewed the work his brother-in-law had done on the sauna during his absence.

Peter had been extremely productive. He'd begun constructing the small platform on which the sauna would sit. After installing the sills on the posts Lund had sunk into the ground, he'd run floor joists from the front to the back and nailed down the small sheets of plywood sub-flooring. Nillson also had finished running the electric line from a junction box inside the cottage to another junction box he'd left dangling on top of the sub-floor.

While Lund admired Nillson's handiwork, his brother-in-law discussed his plans for the framing and the installation of the trusses which would hold up the little shack's peaked roof.

"I can assemble everything on the ground," he said. "Then Anita and Marta can help me lift it into place. They can hold up the wall as I nail it down. The trusses are so small I can handle them myself."

It sounded like a good plan. Lund wished he could help. He might learn something, not that doing handyman work around the house was of major interest to him.

The two couples and the children were lounging outside admiring the slow Swedish sunset, with its rays of red and purple streaking across the horizon out over the lake, when the telephone rang.

Lund stepped back into the cottage to take the call.

It was bad news.

Into Soumi, the fireman from Gothenburg who set the fire in the cathedral the day before, had committed suicide.

Lund quizzed the psychologist who was calling him from the mental health facility in Helsingborg where Soumi had spent the last twenty-four hours of his life. "How could this happen?" Lund didn't wait for an answer. "I thought Mr. Soumi had been placed on suicide watch. I thought the bed sheets had been removed from his room. Earlier today, an aide told me even his shoe laces had been taken away from him."

The psychologist was apologetic. At the same time, however, he made it clear his staff had done everything it could to prevent Soumi's death.

"We have a number of patients here who are on suicide watch," the psychologist explained. "We can't watch all of them all of the time. We did take steps to protect Mr. Soumi. But if people want to kill themselves they will find a way, no matter what we do to prevent it."

Into Soumi had thought of a particularly gruesome way to kill himself.

After his room at the mental-health facility had been cleaned out, only a mattress, a metal bedstead and a small wooden night stand remained. Sometime during the past hour, after the hourly check up by a mental-health aide following dinner, Soumi lay down on the floor under the bed and placed the bottom of one of the bedstead's metal legs on his throat. In this way, he gradually suffocated.

In his time, Lund had investigated dozens of suicides. The method Soumi had chosen was new to him. It must have been an agonizingly slow death. But it was a price the fireman was willing to pay to end his misery.

Lund absolved the psychologist of any blame. "This is not your fault. I guess Mr. Soumi wanted to kill himself so badly he didn't care how he did it. When someone is in that state, I can see there's little you can do about it."

Still, the psychologist felt some responsibility. "I wish I had had a chance to talk more to Mr. Soumi. I'm not sure he was a pyromaniac. His actions at the church yesterday may have been a cry for help. But when he arrived here, he was in a near-cata-tonic state. He wouldn't talk with anyone. I was waiting for him to come around before I tried to sit down with him. Maybe, I should have been more aggressive. It's difficult to know, sometimes."

The phone call put a damper on the rest of the evening for Lund.

The police inspector did a good job of hiding his disappoint-ment at what happened to Soumi from his guests, but Marta knew something was wrong. She always knew. But she didn't say anything until the Nillsons had gone to bed—the children in the tent they had pitched out in front of the cottage and their parents in the addition behind it.

"Are you all right?" Marta asked as she climbed into bed and snuggled up against her husband.

Lund remained silent.

"Was it the telephone call?"

Gradually, Lund rolled over to face his wife. "Yes. It was the phone call."

Marta reached out to touch her husband on the side of his face. "Bad news?"

Lund nodded. "Very bad news."

The police inspector went on to tell his wife of the unfortu-nate tale of Into Soumi. About the fire he'd set in the cathedral in Mareistad. About his brief stay in the mental-health facility in Helsingborg. And about the phone call Lund had received from the psychologist earlier that evening. Finally, he told her about the suicide, leaving out the gruesome details. His wife didn't need to know that.

"What was his name?" Marta asked.

"Soumi," Lund answered. "Into Soumi."

"Soumi? That's a strange name for a Swedish fireman, isn't it? It sounds Finnish."

"Yes," Lund said. "Before he was born, his family emigrated up north to Lulea during the war with Russia."

Lund had missed the war. He was too young. But his older brother, Sven, spent several years as a Marine as part of the mobilization.

"Are his parents still alive?"

"I really don't know. I suppose so. He was relatively young."

"Who is going to tell them?" Marta's voice was filled with concern.

"I don't know." Lund also wondered who would be assigned that unenviable job. Probably some mental health worker in a facility close to the city in northern Sweden where Soumi grew up.

"I hope you don't blame yourself, Magnus," Marta said. "I know how seriously you take these things."

Although Lund felt little guilt for Soumi's suicide, self-doubt had crept in. He wondered whether he had done enough to help the man. If he had spent more time with the young fireman, perhaps things would have been different. Lund's stoic, serious manner often was a good lever for getting suspects to open up. Maybe Soumi would have talked to him.

For a moment, Lund wondered whether his plans to probe the death of the man in the canal were correct. Self-doubt had a way of infecting everything, and he tried to combat it.

"No, I don't blame myself," Lund told his wife. "It's just a sad situation."

Truly, Lund hoped that's all it was. A sad situation.

AFTER COMPLETING his search of Mouse's room, Murphy set out to pick up the trail of the greasy-haired drug dealer.

It took some time.

First, the Army CID investigator checked out the Fox's Den to see whether Mouse had set up shop there.

The bar was packed. On the sound system, CCR had given way to Three Dog Night. Instead of "Bad Moon Rising", it was "Mama Told Me (not to come)." Similar sentiment. Something bad was about to happen.

Because of the music, Murphy guessed the bar was filled with Americans. It was difficult to tell them apart from the Swedes. All the men looked the same. Long hair. Beards or mustaches. Torn faded jeans. Old army field jackets. A haven for hippies.

The two blondes were still there. A half-dozen men hovered around them. But their pretty faces were the only ones familiar to Murphy.

No Reverend Fred. No Ricky Conrad. And definitely no Mouse.

Next, Murphy swept through several cobble-stoned streets closest to the narrow passageway Mouse lived on.

A neighborhood of old stone tenements, the old town district was located on the eastern end of Stadsholmen, one of three small islands which made up the original site of Stockholm.

Again, Murphy came up empty. Mouse wasn't loitering in any of the narrow alleys doing his business.

Then, Murphy walked down to the south end of the island to the stone bridge connecting it with Södermalm, the working-class district to the south.

To the west, Murphy saw the towering spire of the Gothic cathedral dominating the skyline of the small island of Riddarholmen less than a kilometer away. The large buildings near the church appeared devoid of life, so Murphy started walking in the opposite direction along the quay next to Skeppsbron, the wide thoroughfare which arced in a northeasterly direction along the waterfront.

All along the stone pier knots of people, mostly older couples and young families, queued up to board the tour boats about to embark for an evening cruise. As he strolled pass, Murphy picked up snatches of conversation, Swedish. German. Maybe some Danish. But no English. Murphy doubted any of these people were customers of Mouse. They weren't his speed.

As he went along, Murphy looked across to the sidewalk on the opposite side of Skeppsbron. He noticed the building housing the *Expressen*, one of Sweden's top newspapers, but no sign of Mouse.

Murphy walked for perhaps a kilometer before the southern facade of the royal palace came into view. Here, the channel narrowed. On the far bank of the Norstromm, the narrow waterway separating Gamla Stan from the mainland, he could see the flags hanging limp on the roof of the Grand Hotel on the other side of the waterway.

When he reached the palace, Murphy looked west up the broad, cobblestone Slottsbacken. At the top of the incline, no more than two hundred meters away, stood a stone obelisk. Midway in between, Murphy caught a glimpse of the man he had observed following Mouse earlier.

The CID investigator picked up his pace. As he made his way up the hill, Tonto, who Murphy was sure was a Swedish cop, stepped into an opening next to the small orange-hued church across the street from the palace.

Murphy followed, stepping through an open gate into a small courtyard.

To his left, about ten meters away, Mouse sat on a bench under a fruit tree. Not far from him sat the tiny statue of a little boy seated at the edge of a little bowl. The metal sculpture stood no higher than the length of a man's hand.

To his right, Tonto leaned against a wall, perhaps twenty meters across the courtyard from Mouse, his face buried in a tabloid.

The Swedish cop gave no indication he had noticed Murphy. The man's eyes seemed glued to the newspaper, but the CID investigator was sure Tonto didn't miss much of what was happening in the courtyard.

Murphy kept walking across the stone enclosure toward the far wall. The CID investigator adopted the vacant look he used while tailing drug dealers in Philadelphia and New York. He avoided making eye contact with either Mouse or Tonto. He tried to look as if his mind was on something else, not interested in either of them.

Murphy didn't stop. He kept on walking, exiting the small courtyard through an opening in the back wall. He turned right and ambled up a narrow alley in the direction of the Storkyrkan, the large sandstone-colored church that sat on the island's highest point.

A few moments later, Murphy took up residence on the narrow stone outcropping at the base of a statue of King Frederick. The statue sat in a niche in a back wall of the church across the square from the entrance to the courtyard of the Finnish church.

The CID investigator tried to appear comfortable in his strange surroundings. He tried to look like he belonged there. It wasn't easy.

Moments after Murphy sat down, he was joined by a heavily made-up, gray-haired woman old enough to be his mother.

Murphy pulled out his cigarettes. "Do you mind if I smoke?"

He spoke just loud enough for only the woman to hear. He showed her the pack of Rothmans. "Is it okay?"

Responding with a heavily-accented "okay," the old woman reached for a cigarette. She had misunderstood his gesture.

Murphy shrugged. He took out two cigarettes. After handing one to the woman, he finally got his Zippo to spark. He lit both of them.

As the smoke swirled around him, Murphy sat back on the bench, stretched out his legs, and took a long drag.

Turning toward the woman, Murphy held up his smoke. "Okay?"

The old woman smiled. Her teeth were stained and yellowed. "Okay," she answered.

Wearing a grin of his own he asked her, "You don't speak English, do you?"

She smiled again. "Okay," was all she said.

Murphy nodded. "That's what I thought."

That was the end of their conversation.

For Mouse, it was business as usual.

During the first fifteen minutes Murphy sat watching the entrance to the courtyard, only three people—two young men and a skinny blonde woman—went into it. The visitors left the little stone enclosure the same way they went in, after an interval of perhaps no more than a minute.

Murphy estimated each exchange was completed in a matter of seconds. Pretty slick.

It was not a good situation for Murphy. After smoking his second cigarette, he realized he really didn't have a good reason to remain seated on the bench below the statue of the pudgy Hessian prince who ruled Sweden with a relatively soft touch for about three decades nearly three centuries before.

Other than to check out the young druggies who visited

Mouse, it really wasn't a place to watch people. Murphy was sure his perch was purely ornamental and he would draw attention to himself by sitting there for a long period of time.

For the first time in a long time, Murphy felt an odd sensation. He was alone, with no backup, walking out on the edge. He didn't feel in danger, but he did feel he was close to blowing this assignment.

Back in the States, when he worked similar details, Murphy usually was part of a team. Normally, it would take a squad of three or four men to maintain a tail. Working alone on those assignments, it was a recipe for disaster. The quarry makes you for a tail once, and your cover is blown.

No matter how dumb Mouse looked, it could occur even to him after a while he was being followed.

Murphy sensed it was time to change tack. The long slow dusk was settling in, and the light was starting to fade in front of the statue.

It occurred to Murphy the Swedish cop was following Mouse for the same reason he was. At least three drug deals had gone down in front of him, and Tonto apparently hadn't made a move.

Murphy thought about what he had found during his search of the room. The small stash of drugs. The backpack. The dirty laundry. They were all signs the little drug dealer hadn't taken up permanent residence in Stockholm.

Maybe, there was no good reason for Murphy to follow Mouse around Gamla Stan.

Murphy decided to break off the tail.

From what the CID investigator had learned from his search, he was sure Mouse's time in Stockholm was growing short. He was about to run out of drugs to push.

All Murphy had to know was when Mouse was leaving. Then, he could resume his tail.

Murphy lit another cigarette. When he did, he heard the woman murmur "okay." He fished out one for her. As he lit it, Mouse walked out of the entrance to the courtyard. No more than ten seconds later, the Swedish cop, with his folded newspaper tucked under his arm, walked out. Tonto stopped, unfolded his newspaper, and began reading it again while leaning against a stone wall.

Murphy stayed put.

From where he sat, the CID investigator watched as Mouse walked in the direction of the Stortorget, heading back into the heart of Gamla Stan.

Murphy waited.

About ten seconds later, after Mouse had moved out of sight, the Swedish cop began walking, resuming his stalking. Murphy admired the way the Swede worked. It was an easy laid-back approach. He was just keeping tabs.

After Tonto disappeared from his view, Murphy turned and walked back down Slottsbacken in the opposite direction.

At the bottom of the hill, Murphy turned right onto Skeppsbron and strolled back along the sidewalk to Reverend Fred's apartment.

He was sure Mouse wasn't going anywhere that night. He still had drugs left to sell in his stash.

Murphy just had to be ready to roll when he made his move.

BY THE TIME GUNDERSON arrived to pick him up for the drive to Stockholm, Inspector Lund had shaved, showered, devoured a breakfast of kippers and donned his bathing trunks.

Lund had tried to do all of that without waking his niece and nephew.

He failed.

At first light, Britta and Arvid crawled out of their sleeping bags and began to hound Lund. Still wearing their pajamas, the two youngsters peppered Lund with questions.

"Can we sail today, Uncle Magnus?" Arvid asked.

"I don't know," Lund answered.

"Will the boat float?" Britta queried.

"We'll see," Lund promised.

"Will you set up the rigging?" his nephew inquired.

Good question.

"I'll think about it," his uncle answered.

By the time Gunderson arrived, Arvid and Britta had finally run out of questions. That was good. Lund had run out of answers.

After Gunderson changed into his swim trunks, the two men waded into the water.

"Damn! It's cold!" Gunderson said, his teeth chattering, as he trudged through the chilly, placid waters of the big lake.

Lund chuckled. "Dive in! You'll feel better." Taking his own advice, Lund took a few running steps and propelled himself into a shallow dive. Ten meters from the shore, his head bobbed to the surface. "I shouldn't have bothered to shower," he exclaimed. "This is invigorating."

Following the police inspector's lead, Gunderson also ran

forward and knifed through the surface of the water.

The sunken sailing dinghy sat in more than a meter of water, and the two men had to wrestle with it for several minutes before they were able to turn the little boat on its side.

"God, that's a workout," Gunderson breathed.

Another chuckle came from Lund. "We're not done yet. Push."

The two men leaned forward and flipped the boat completely over.

Because the weight of the water no longer pinned the dinghy to the lake bottom, the two men were able to lift it slightly and gradually muscle it into the shallow water closer to the beach. Finally, after much exertion, the sailboat was turned to an upright position. Then, Lund gave the little wooden boat a push back into the lake. It floated.

It took a few more minutes to rig the dinghy to sail. First, Lund and Gunderson stepped in the wooden mast near the bow of the cat-rigged boat and attached the much shorter boom to it. Then, Lund tugged on the little metal lever at the bottom of the trunk amidships to make sure the centerboard deployed. It did. Next, he fastened a length of rope attached to a small metal ring in the bow.

After tying the canvas sail bag to a cleat near the stern and putting the little wooden tiller and two lifejackets into the cockpit, he issued his sailing orders to his niece and nephew.

"Rule number one, don't sail out of sight of the cottage," he intoned. "I don't want to have to fetch you from the other side of the bay when I return from Stockholm."

Lund continued. "The best time to sail today will be around noon. There should be a slight breeze coming in from the west. You will have to tack out into it. Try to angle the boat slightly when you jib into the wind. I don't want you to overturn the boat and go for a swim in the middle of the bay. You understand?"

Arvid and Britta nodded in agreement.

"Good," Lund said.

With that, the two policemen left for the drive to Stockholm. While Gunderson drove, Lund buried his face into the Martin Beck mystery he had started to read two days before.

For the most part, the young police patrolman kept his eyes on the road. Only once, very early in the trip, did Gunderson complain about taking his Audi to Stockholm.

"If we had The Rocket, we could cut a lot of time off the drive," he said.

Lund looked up from his book. "I wanted to take an unmarked car, but the department doesn't have one," he explained. "If we arrive in the Dodge, we might attract the attention of the Stockholm police. Perhaps they'd ask some questions I'd rather not answer. Right now, I really don't want them to know why we're in Stockholm. I want to keep a low profile. You understand?"

Apparently, Gunderson understood. He didn't say another word.

For the rest of the trip, the young policeman focused on his driving, and Lund kept turning the pages of the crime novel.

Only thirty pages into the book, the police inspector was trying to figure out what the title *Polis polis potatismos* had to do with the murder of a well-known businessman while he was dining at the posh Savoy Hotel in Malmo.

It seemed to be a play on words of the common rhyme, *Polis, polis potatisgris*. In the book title, authors Sjowall and Wahloo had changed the words "potato pig" at the end of the rhyme to "mashed potatoes." Why? Lund didn't know. Not yet.

Lund had already read the first five books in the Beck series. The two Swedish writers had a penchant for titling their books with an obscure reference to the plot. At some point during his reading, he would discover the connection.

Polis, polis potatismos was one book his wife Marta wasn't going to read with her husband.

She didn't like to read mystery novels, especially those which had a Swedish police inspector as its main character. "I have my own Swedish police inspector at home," she joked.

Earlier that summer, the Lunds had read *The French Lieutenant's Woman,* by the British author John Fowles. In English. The year before, the romance novel, set in Victorian England, had been an international best seller.

Fowles' book was too literary for Lund's taste. It concluded with the author offering three alternative endings. That was two too many for Lund. The police inspector liked to read books with conclusions which left no room for doubt.

That's why the Beck series appealed to Lund. Often, Sjowall and Wahloo took a circuitous route, but the writing team always provided a satisfying ending to their crime novels.

About halfway to Stockholm, Lund wondered how the case he was working on would end.

Would it have a satisfactory conclusion?

He wondered whether he had taken the right tack. After all, his superiors didn't even know he was working on a murder case.

What would Martin Beck do in this situation? Often, during his investigations, the fictional Swedish police inspector bucked authority in his pursuit of the truth. Lund thought about that for a while. By the time he reached Stockholm, he was convinced the fictional police inspector would approve of his approach.

The Swedish Immigration Board was located on Fredsgatan in central Stockholm in one of the old, classically-designed office buildings near Parliament.

Gunderson grew up in Sigtuna, a historic town just north of the Swedish capital. He had spent enough time in Stockholm playing ice hockey and chasing women to know his way around. When they reached the outskirts, the young patrolman left the highway and skirted the traffic in the city's center by taking a meandering route through back streets to get Lund to his appointment on time.

S. Waldman, the immigration board official with whom Lund had made an appointment, turned out to be a pretty young woman. Her name was Sofia. An ash blonde with sparkling green eyes, she was all business when the two policeman sat down to talk with her.

Lund liked that. The police inspector got to the point. He told her about the dead man found floating in the Göta Canal. Then he explained the significance of the Globe and Anchor tattoo found on the left arm of the corpse.

The young woman understood. "So you think he was an American marine. An American citizen." It was a statement, not a question.

Lund nodded. Then he removed a copy of the composite drawing of the dead man from his briefcase and slid it across the desk to her. "Here's what we think he looked like, Miss Waldman. We thought your organization might help us identify him."

A slight pause followed these statements. "It is Miss, isn't it?"

Lund was right. It was Miss Waldman. She affirmed it with a nod and a smile. Her friendly grin lasted only a moment before she again adopted her serious official expression.

After studying the portrait for a few seconds, Miss Waldman wore a puzzled expression. "I don't know how much help I can be."

That comment caught Lund by surprise. For a moment he wondered if the trip to Stockholm had been a waste of time. He had no time to waste, especially in this case.

"Doesn't your department process all of the American military deserters who enter Sweden?" he asked.

Waldman nodded. "Yes, it does."

"Doesn't your department photograph each one of the deserters when they make application to live in Sweden?"

Another nod. "We do."

"Can't we look at those photos and see if we can find a match?"

To Lund, it seemed a simple request.

He was wrong.

Waldman shook her pretty head.

"No," she said. "That is not allowed. It is confidential information, and the police are not allowed to see those photos."

Waldman said the no-look policy was adopted when the board was formed three years before to handle the influx of immigrants into Sweden to help meet the labor needs of the nation's burgeoning economy.

"Not all policemen support our policy of opening Sweden to people from the outside, and we don't want them to harass the newcomers," she explained. "Some Swedish policemen have disdain for those men who have deserted from the American military because of the Vietnam War."

On that issue, Lund remained truly neutral.

As a policeman, a public servant, he believed it was none of his business who came to live in Sweden. At least not until they ran afoul of the law. Only then would he stick his nose into their affairs.

The police inspector was unsure where Gunderson stood on the issue. It didn't take long for him to learn of the young patrolman's feelings about the American deserters. Discretion was not a strong suit of his.

Up to this point, the young patrolman had been sitting quietly next to Lund, his dark brown eyes focused on the pretty young woman sitting across the desk from him watching her talk to Lund, a pleasant smile plastered on his handsome face. When the talk turned to the American deserters, his expression changed. It became serious as he joined the conversation.

"I think they should line up all of those deserters and shoot them," Gunderson blurted. "They're all traitors."

Miss Waldman smiled. "That sounds a bit harsh, doesn't it, officer?"

Her smile was disarming, and it forced the young patrolman to back off. A little.

"Well, maybe, they shouldn't be shot," he said. "But I don't think life should be made comfortable for them here."

Miss Waldman politely disagreed. "It is official policy," she said. "As long as they make an effort to become good Swedes, the government guarantees the immigrants will have the same living standards enjoyed by most citizens. It is the law."

Neutrality was not a way of life for all Swedes. As Lund could see, Miss Waldman and Officer Gunderson held opposing views regarding the United States military deserters, while he was stuck in the middle.

Lund returned to the point of the meeting.

"Look, Miss Waldman, we didn't come here to argue about government policy." The police inspector pointed at the composite sitting on the desk. "We need your help. Surely, there is a way for you to help us determine the identity of this man."

Miss Waldman glanced at the picture. "Perhaps I can have one of clerks compare it to the photographs in our files." She picked up the drawing. "You think he is one of the American deserters?"

Lund nodded. "It seems plausible. His tattoo—the Globe and Anchor—would indicate that is possible."

Miss Waldman placed the composite back on the her desk. "I will attend to that. If we find anything, I will call you."

Lund and Gunderson stood up to leave.

"Is there anything else I can help you with?" Miss Waldman asked.

After a moment's thought, it occurred to Lund there was something else Miss Waldman could do for him.

"Well, Officer Gunderson and I did travel a long way to get here, and we would like the trip to be worthwhile," he answered. "I was wondering if you knew someone else we could see while we were in Stockholm who may be of help to us? Another government official? Perhaps, even an American."

Miss Waldman thumbed through a small metal file box on her desk.

"There is someone I know who might be able to help you," she said.

After studying the contents of the white index card she pulled from the box, the immigration official scribbled on a notepad on her desk. "Here's his name and address." She handed the slip of paper to Lund.

Lund looked at what was written.

"This is not a Swedish name," he stated.

"No, he's an American," she explained. "He works with the Army deserters from West Germany."

The address was unfamiliar to the police inspector.

Lund showed the note to Gunderson.

"Do you know where this is?"

"Yes," Gunderson smiled. "It's in Gamla Stan. The old town."

"Is it close by?"

"A short walk," Gunderson assured Lund. "Just over the bridge. Not far from the royal palace."

The visit with Miss Waldman had come to an end.

"Let's take a walk then," Lund suggested.

"I know a shortcut," Gunderson said.

MURPHY AWOKE TO FIND Reverend Fred in the kitchenette leaning over a large pot of boiling water on the small electric range.

Burgess pointed to the cubes of meat stacked on a cutting board next to the stove. "Venison. One of my Swedish friends shot a doe up north. I'm making a stew."

The apron the young minister wore was much too short for his tall, lanky body.

Murphy looked at the meat. "Kind of warm for stew, isn't it?"

Tiny beads of sweat had formed on Burgess' forehead. "I don't have any choice." He picked up the cutting board and slid the little cubes into the bubbling water. "If I don't do something with it, the meat will spoil."

On the small counter next to the stove were piles of diced potatoes, celery stalks, pearl onions, bunches of parsnips and carrots.

While Reverend Fred worked on the stew, Murphy retreated to the communal bath. Located off the landing between the second and third floors of the old apartment building, it contained a small sink, a commode and an old claw-foot bathtub. Murphy didn't bother to shave. He wanted to maintain his grubby look. But he did take a bath. There was no shower.

Sliding into the tub as it filled with hot water, Murphy felt a familiar stab of pain in his left side when he rubbed against the porcelain of the narrow tub. It felt like a bee sting, but it was much more than that. It was a reminder of the nugget-sized chunk of shrapnel a Navy doctor in Phu Bai had dug out of his left kidney after a mortar round exploded near him during the Tet Offensive more than three years before.

Two or three times a year, a little remnant of the mortar round worked its way out through his skin. For the past year, Kate used a set of tweezers and her gentle touch to wiggle the thin piece of metal out. Then, she would kiss the spot. Murphy liked that. This time, the little piece of metal, barely the size of a finger nail clipping would have to wait. Hopefully, Kate would still want to perform her magic with her tweezers when he got back home.

Murphy had gotten a fitful night of sleep, listening to Conrad snore and fart on the cot next to him in the apartment's cramped bedroom.

The young deserter got drunk the night before. Maybe he was celebrating his separation from the Army. Maybe not. Murphy didn't know and he didn't care.

The two men shared the same room. But they had nothing else in common. Neither spoke to the other. Not even a hello or good-bye passed between them.

If the situation were different, and Murphy didn't have to maintain his cover, he would have hauled Conrad in. Trouble was in Sweden there was no place to haul his ass to. The Swedes had allowed Conrad, as well as hundreds of other deserters, to take up residence. All of them lived under the protection of the Swedish government, which had adopted its traditional neutral stance in the Vietnam War. Uncle Sam could try to persuade the deserters to return to the fold, but he couldn't haul their young asses anywhere.

That was especially frustrating for Murphy. For now, it was best he didn't talk much to Conrad. He didn't want to blow his cover by losing his cool.

It was different with Burgess. At least Reverend Fred and the CID investigator were civil to one another. If the young minister had gotten a hint of Murphy's animosity toward the other boarder in his cramped apartment, he didn't let on.

Still, Murphy remained guarded in his comments to the young minister. He didn't want to give him an inkling of who he was and what he was really up to.

Burgess seemed to buy Murphy's story. To the young minister, the CID investigator appeared to be one step above a bum. He didn't want to give Reverend Fred any reason to think differently.

Burgess was unlike the other clergymen Murphy had known.

By the time Murphy had climbed into the cot to go to sleep the night before, Burgess hadn't returned to the apartment.

Murphy didn't go to church much. Not anymore. But his mother did.

His experience with men of the cloth was limited to the priests at the little Catholic church on Cape Cod his mother attended every Sunday.

Murphy didn't recall any of the priests staying out all night.

He also didn't think any of them would know the first thing about making deer stew. The old women in the small Massachusetts parish usually did the cooking for them.

The young minister didn't make breakfast for Murphy. Instead, he offered him a large bowl of Cheerios, enlivened with a handful of raspberries.

"My little sister sent me a care package," Burgess explained. "Cheerios are my favorite."

Right after breakfast, Murphy set out to find Mouse.

So far, Mouse was Murphy's only possible lead in his search for Marlon Andrews, the killer he'd been sent to Sweden to find.

At least he was in the same business as Fish. Murphy doubted many Americans pushed dope in Sweden. Not if they wanted to remain in the country or stay out of jail.

Andrews could be involved in the trade. Mouse could be a link.

It was worth Murphy's time to check him out.

Murphy headed down the hill to Stora Nygatan and walked to Mouse's room.

His door was padlocked.

The little drug dealer was out.

After climbing up the narrow stone steps to Västerlänggatan, he checked out the Fox's Den.

No Mouse. Just a couple of old barflies sitting at the bar getting an early start on the day.

Continuing his search, Murphy took a left onto Kingstugatan. After walking past the tall copper-spired, red-brick German Church, he kept walking east until he reached the large bronze statue of St. George brandishing his sword as he prepared to slay a dragon while sitting astride his sturdy steed. Here, Murphy took another left and headed back up the hill in the direction of the Finnish Church, where Mouse had spent time pushing drugs the day before.

Murphy missed his mark. Instead of winding up in front of the little orange-colored stone church, he walked into Stortorget, the public square in front of the Swedish Academy in the center of Gamla Stan.

The tall, narrow stone buildings surrounding the square were painted a riot of colors. Reds, greens, ochre, orange. It was very different from the brownstones Murphy was used to seeing in Boston. For a moment he was taken aback.

While regaining his bearings, Murphy stood next to an impressive piece of stonework, a memorial to the group of Swedish noblemen and clergymen massacred on that spot in 1520 by the conquering Danes in what became known as the Stockholm Bloodbath. Murphy heard band music.

From the square, Murphy headed north down Kallargrand toward the royal palace. As he walked past the tall stone obelisk which dominated the square in front of the old stock exchange building, a group of uniformed musicians marched up Slottsbacken toward him. In the band's wake trailed a platoon of blue-clad soldiers.

It was the start of the daily changing of the palace guard.

Keeping to the right side of the wide cobblestone street, Murphy headed down the hill toward the Northbro Bridge. He watched as the small military band and the platoon of soldiers with rifles slung from their shoulders marched past him.

The contingent of Swedish soldiers wore shiny spiked helmets reminiscent of the headgear worn by generations of Prussian soldiers. The heels of their shoes clicked on the cobblestones as they slowly marched past him, but the soldiers seemed to lack the precise, intricate movements employed by the U.S. Army's Old Guard during the changing of the guard ceremony at the Tomb of The Unknowns at Arlington National Cemetery.

To Murphy, it looked like the Swedish soldiers were simply pulling guard duty. It was no big deal to them. The music, which reverberated off the stone buildings, filled the air. But there seemed to be little emotion surrounding the ceremony. It was a show.

As he watched the Swedish soldiers slowly make their way around the corner to the entrance of the palace's outer courtyard, Murphy's mind drifted to Van Dyck.

V.D. was buried at Arlington. But Murphy wasn't thinking about that, nor about the trips he'd taken down to D.C. to visit his old friend's grave in the vast garden of stone.

No.

He was wondering what Van Dyck would do in his situation.

Murphy already knew the answer.

"Follow your nose." Time and time again, the old warrant officer had told him. "Go where it takes you. It never lets you down."

While working a case, Murphy relied heavily on his intuition. From Van Dyck, he'd learned the finer points of police work. How to build an inventory of evidence. How to check and re-check the facts. How to tell when someone was telling the truth, or better yet, when they were not. Good stuff. All of it essential in building an iron-clad case.

However, it was Murphy's uncanny knack of picking up the scent of a suspect, the gut feeling he had when he got on the trail of someone, which enabled him to close most of his investigations.

"You got a gift," Van Dyck often told him. "Use it!"

Right now, Murphy's gut was telling him the items he had found during his search of Mouse's room pointed in one direction. The drugs. The wad of cash. The suitcase. It all told him Mouse was working for somebody else.

At some point, Mouse was leaving town. Where was he going?

But Murphy couldn't spend all his time following Mouse around Stockholm. Somewhere along the line, someone was going to notice him. Maybe Tonto would make him. It was even possible Mouse would figure out someone was tailing him, sooner or later.

The CID investigator needed help.

But Murphy couldn't break cover.

"No matter what, don't let anyone get under your cover," Van Dyck often warned Murphy. "Don't let anyone know who you really are. It's too dangerous. You could get hurt."

It was good advice then. It was good advice now.

After the soldiers marched out of sight, Murphy remained at his spot on Slottsbacken just down the hill from the Finnish church.

A few minutes after the parade passed, a phalanx of Swedish policemen walked up the hill. They wore riot gear. Helmets. Shields. They carried batons.

A mob walked behind the line of cops.

At the front of the group, several marchers carried a long red banner. On it, emblazoned in large white letters were the words *Fred Och Karlek*. At both ends of the banner, peace signs had been painted in white.

After the few hundred antiwar protesters moved in amoeba-like fashion up Slottsbacken, the policemen subtly directed them to the left, opposite the route the soldiers had taken to the rear of the palace.

To Murphy, it was clear. The peaceniks would be allowed to hold their protest. But they would not be allowed to interfere with the traditional ceremonies taking place in the palace courtyard.

Following the path of least resistance, the protesters moved near the Storkyrkan.

Murphy fit right in with the peace marchers with his goatee and four-day growth. His long, curly hair falling over the collar of his well-worn Army field jacket. His faded blue jeans. His beat-up work boots. He had the look nailed down.

Murphy's sympathies lay elsewhere.

He didn't think such demonstrations would bring a speedy end to the war in South Vietnam.

He also doubted the peace movement did much to improve the morale of the soldiers still stuck in South Vietnam fighting it.

At this point, he doubted there was little anyone could do to bolster their spirits.

Murphy agreed every one had a right to march in protest. Here in Sweden. Back in the U.S. Everywhere. He just didn't see the point of it.

Murphy doubted President Nixon was moved by such gestures. The CID investigator wasn't.

A few moments after the final demonstrators surrounded the stone obelisk at the top of the hill, knots of people, mostly families with young children, streamed up Slottsbacken. From their dress, it was clear none of them were participating in the protest. A lot of the adults carried cameras. The cops allowed these people to move in the direction of the palace. They walked quickly to catch up with the soldiers.

Murphy took a step across the street to follow the tourists to the large baroque palace when something caught his eye. Trotting up the hill was Mouse. A waif-like blonde girl clung to his arm.

Murphy waited. As the couple passed by, he heard her say "Mus."

Her soft voice sounded familiar. He was sure it was the girl from the hallway.

The CID investigator couldn't make out the string of heavily-accented English words which followed. But Mouse could. In response, Mouse gave her a little peck on the cheek followed by a reassuring pat on her bony ass.

Before Murphy fell in behind Mouse and his little girlfriend, he checked himself.

Murphy wasn't worried about Mouse figuring out he was being followed. Mouse didn't seem to care. He acted as if he was oblivious to the world around him.

But Murphy was concerned about something else. He wondered whether the Swedish cop was still tailing Mouse. The CID investigator didn't want to be spotted by him.

Before he moved from his position near the Finnish Church, Murphy surveyed the route Mouse and the girl had just taken up the hill.

Murphy reached into his pocket for his box of Rothmans. Cupping his hand over his mouth as he lit a cigarette, he glanced back down the hill from between his splayed fingers.

By the time Murphy zeroed in on Tonto, the Swedish cop was halfway up Slottsbacken. This time, he wore a leather jacket and carried a Canon 35-millimeter camera with a telephoto lens on a strap draped around his neck. Nice touch, thought Murphy. Tonto looked like a tourist, but he still had the same determined expression from the day before.

As the young Swedish cop strode by, Murphy avoided eye contact. He also refrained from making any gestures which might draw attention to him. He didn't make a move. He became a statue.

Murphy didn't want to risk being uncovered by a Swedish policeman, so he decided to change tactics.

Instead of maintaining his tail on Mouse, the CID investigator would follow the young Swedish cop. Tonto would help him keep tabs on the little drug dealer. Remaining outside the direct line of sight between Mouse and his Swedish tail should reduce the risk.

After a few minutes, the CID investigator left his position near the little stone church. He slowly walked up the hill, moving in the same direction as Mouse and the Swedish cop.

As Murphy closed in on the mob surrounding the stone obelisk in front of the old stock exchange building, he took one last look down the hill behind him. He wanted to make sure Tonto was working alone. The CID investigator didn't want the Lone Ranger covering his faithful companion's back. He remained rooted to a spot not far from one of the little wooden guard shacks next to the royal palace until he was sure no masked man was walking up Slottsbacken.

As Murphy glanced back, he couldn't pick out anyone. No

one around him was walking alone. Lots of young couples with their kids. Elderly couples with each other. But no singles. No one looked like he or she didn't belong there.

Murphy was sure there was not another tail in the group of people trudging up the hill behind him.

But he did notice something else.

Three black women walked up Slottsbacken.

Two of them wore dresses similar to the long skirts he'd seen women wear while he was on an assignment in Ethiopia three years before.

The woman who walked between the pair, wearing a short black skirt and a white blouse, looked quite familiar.

Murphy forgot about Mouse and Tonto. He even forgot about Fish.

None of them mattered. At least, for now.

Only one question was on Murphy's mind.

What was Romana Alley doing in Sweden?

MARLON ANDREWS sat at a small table next to the mill pond picking at a garden salad.

"Jhonas, I swear you can't get a leaf of lettuce anywhere in this country," Fish complained, spearing a chunk of celery with his fork.

Across the table sat Jhonas, the head of the commune where the American had found refuge after arriving in Sweden the year before.

"Marlon, I don't think we ever developed a taste for lettuce," Jhonas said. "Until recently, it was extremely difficult to store lettuce during the winter months, and so we Swedes grew vegetables that could be pickled to eat during our long winters."

Fish grunted.

"But I didn't come to see you today to talk about Swedish cuisine," his host said.

"That's what I like about you, Jhonas," said Andrews, looking up from his salad. "You always get right to the point."

It had been that way since the first night the men met in a bar in Gothenburg.

Andrews had told the tall blond Swede, who spoke nearly perfect English, that he needed a place to crash after his discharge from the United States Army in West Germany. Jhonas said he needed a caretaker for some property he owned outside the town of Laxa.

From the start of their relationship, only first names were used. It was always Jhonas, and it was always Marlon. Fish liked that.

Later, Marlon met Jakob, a body builder, and Tomas, the commune's music expert.

Over time, Fish also met a cadre of women that seemed to change with the seasons.

This morning, Ingrid, a dark-haired beauty who joined the group during its recent month-long stay in Spain, assembled the salad Fish was eating.

The group traveled a lot.

The previous winter, after meeting the American, Jhonas took his troupe on an expedition down the east coast of Africa. For nearly two months, they traveled in his microbus, which had been shipped to Mombasa, through Kenya and Tanzania.

While the group was gone, Andrews kept an eye on the commune, located about five kilometers outside Laxa off the road to Karlskoga, another small industrial city about forty kilometers to the north.

While Jhonas and his band of young men and women occupied the main house, a large two-story wooden structure, Andrews lived in a cabin next to the mill pond.

Jhonas had inherited the property. His great-grandfather developed the saw mill, which now lay abandoned at the far end of the mill pond, and gradually amassed holdings of more than a thousand hectares of woodland. After the war, his parents sold off the bulk of the forestland and set up a trust for their son, their only child. They lived in Stockholm and seldom visited the family's former summer home, which Jhonas converted into a year-round residence after he started drawing from the trust.

"When we met, I said you could stay here as long as you kept your nose clean," Jhonas said. "Jakob and Tomas have both told me you've been selling drugs."

Andrews put down his fork. "You got a problem with that?" He gestured toward the main house. "You and your friends smoke pot all the time."

Jhonas nodded. "I know," he paused for a moment. "But it's

different with us, Marlon. We cultivate cannabis in small plots out in the woods, out of sight. We grow marijuana for ourselves, and give some to our friends. But we don't sell it."

As the two men talked, a couple of sparrows took turns flitting down to the table from the hedge that screened the camp from the main house. Andrews had placed a few kernels of corn, some black beans and soybeans on a small saucer next to his plate, and each of the little birds would land for a few seconds and peck at the food. The sparrows showed up whenever the American ate outside.

Andrews shrugged. "So what do you want me to do?"

Jhonas sat back in his chair. "Maybe, it's time for you to leave."

Another sparrow dropped in and pecked at a kernel of corn.

"I don't want to get into trouble," Jhonas explained. "Right now, the cops leave us alone because we don't cause problems. All we do is smoke some pot. But you're selling anything you can get your hands on, and that could mean trouble for us."

Andrews gestured with his fork as he resumed eating. "I know, this wasn't part of the deal," he said. "But I've been very careful. I've had guys on the street selling the stuff in Stockholm and Gothenburg. Nowhere near here."

Andrews had brought a large stash of drugs with him when he left West Germany, but he didn't tell Jhonas that his cache was nearly depleted. He just needed a little more time to get rid of all of it.

"My guys are cautious," Fish told Jhonas. "They're real pros."

Jhonas shook his head. "I don't care how cautious they are," he said. "They're going to make one mistake, and the police will trail them here, and we'll get into trouble. I don't want that to happen."

Another sparrow chirped as it flew down to the table to take the place of its partner.

"Well, how long do I have?" Andrews seemed resigned to the ultimatum he'd just been given. "When do I have to clear out of here?"

Jhonas announced a deadline. "Later today we're driving south to go to the music festival in Karlshamn," he said. "We'll be gone three, four days. When we get back we don't want to find you here, Marlon. Understood?"

"Yeah, I get it," Andrews nodded reluctantly. "I don't like it, but I get it."

The two little sparrows again exchanged places bobbing for food while standing next to the saucer a few inches away from Andrews's plate.

Jhonas stood up to leave. "By the way, are you going out the same way you came in?"

Andrews was noncommittal. "You know, I can't tell you that."

Jhonas nodded. "That's a good policy. That way I don't have to lie should the police come here. I don't like to lie to the police. That's a bad policy."

Andrews knew he had no choice but to leave by the same route he had entered the country. While he had been in Sweden, he let his hair grow long. He also had cultivated a beard and began sporting a small silver ring on his right ear lobe.

Before he could leave, Andrews would have to change his look again.

Fish didn't like that. This wasn't part of his plan. It made him angry.

As Jhonas walked away, another sparrow swooped in and landed next to the plate, bypassing the meal that had been set aside for the birds on the saucer.

Andrews glanced down at the table.

In one deft move, Fish swept in with his right hand and plucked the little brown bird off the table. While holding his arm outstretched, he balled his hand into a tight fist.

When Andrews unclenched his fist, the bird fell to the ground. It was dead.

MURPHY HAD little difficulty recognizing Romana, but it was different for her.

"Ciao, Romana," he had called out, trailing a few steps behind the three women. "Remember me?"

The three women stopped and turned. Each wore a puzzled expression.

First, Romana spoke in Svenska.

Murphy was taken aback. He didn't expect to hear her spout Swedish. Quickly, he recovered. "Sorry, I don't understand a word. What did you say?"

Romana switched to her lightly-accented English. "I said, 'Excuse me. Do I know you?' " Before continuing, she said a few words in her native Tigrinya to her two puzzled companions. "Your voice sounds familiar." She gazed intently at Murphy. "But I just can't place your face."

It was understandable. Murphy didn't look anything like the relatively clean-cut CID investigator Romana had met in Asmara three years before. His hair was much longer. He also wore a goatee, and his grizzled look was enhanced by the week-old growth. The old Army field jacket and faded jeans completed Murphy's unkempt appearance. He looked like a bum. A hippie. Just like Smith said.

"It's John," he said. "John Murphy. Don't you remember me?"

After Romana studied his face for a few more moments, a spark of recognition replaced her look of bewilderment. Her eyes lit up.

"Ah, I can see that now." A warmth quite familiar to Murphy replaced her initial wariness. "John Murphy, my old friend from America. It is you."

Romana rushed into Murphy's arms, hugging him. Reflexively, he leaned forward. He put his arms around her.

As they hugged, the CID investigator took a close look at Romana.

The skin on Romana's pretty face was still wrinkle-free, but it had become taut. Her expression seemed severe. The set to her large deep brown eyes had hardened.

The color of Romana's skin seemed to have darkened. She no longer had the light brown sugar hue she had when Murphy first met her while riding on the Littorina down the mountain to Massawa.

As Murphy held her, Romana's tiny body felt even thinner than it had the last time they embraced. But her hold was firm as she stood on her tiptoes to put her arms around him.

It was clear to Murphy. Romana had weathered some tough times during the past three years. She had lost some of her youthful luster. Still, her smile remained as radiant as ever as she looked up to gaze at him.

Romana seemed glad to see him, and Murphy felt the same.

Apparently, the bond forged during the five intense days they spent together three years before was still tight. It appeared to be one of those friendships which could be picked up right where it left off.

And where was that?

Romana stopped writing him. Murphy met Kate. Romana—like most of the other women in his life—was placed on the back burner. Permanently.

Now, here Murphy and Romana were, facing each other while a peace demonstration took place near the Swedish royal palace thousands of miles from their homes.

Almost simultaneously, they posed the same question: "What are you doing here?"

Before either of them could answer, their reunion was interrupted by a string of Tigrinya from one of Romana's companions.

"What did she say?" Murphy asked.

Romana smiled. "She wonders if you are one of my long-lost lovers."

After withdrawing from the embrace, Romana spoke to the two women. In Tigrinya. As she spoke, their faces lit up. Each smiled warmly at Murphy.

The reactions of the two African women puzzled Murphy. "What did you tell them?"

Romana smiled. "I told them none of my lovers are lost. Every one of them knows exactly where he is."

Then, after Romana said a few more words in Tigrinya, the two women walked off. After a few steps, one of them turned to look back at Murphy. Smiling broadly, she gave a little wave. "Bye Bye," she said, in heavily-accented English.

Murphy returned her wave.

Romana linked an arm with one of his and gently guided Murphy around the periphery of the demonstration and headed back down Kallargrand toward the near-empty Stortorget. "I told my friends I would meet them later at our apartment," she explained, as they neared a bench in front of the Swedish Academy. "Now, you must tell me what you are doing here in Sweden."

Murphy had always been open with Romana. She was someone he could trust, even with the secretive nature of his current assignment.

"I'm working a case," he explained. "I'm looking for a man, a killer."

As they sat down, Murphy went on to tell Romana about Marlon Andrews. He included every detail he knew about the crimes

Fish had committed in West Germany. "We think he came to Sweden to hide out among the American deserters."

Then, Murphy told Romana about Mouse. About the drugs and money he'd uncovered in the little American drug pusher's room. "I've been trying to keep track of him." He glanced in the direction of the Royal Palace, which was now out of his sight. "The last time I saw him he was heading toward those hippies and freaks."

The peace protest was in full swing. From where they sat, they could hear the crowd's chants of "Peace Now!" echoing off the stone walls of the buildings in the Kallergrand, the wide alley which connected the two main squares in Gamla Stan.

"Oh, I must let you go then." Romana sounded truly apologetic. "I must not interfere with your work."

Murphy reached out to touch Romana's arm. "Don't worry. It can wait."

Ordinarily, nothing stood between Murphy and his assignment. He was a professional, unrelenting in his approach. Ordinarily. But this was different. For the moment, he forgot about his search for Marlon Andrews and the exact whereabouts of Mouse. For the moment.

Romana was more important.

What was she doing in Sweden?

Not long after they had reached the square and taken a seat on one of the iron benches in front of the Swedish Academy, Murphy lit a cigarette.

Romana chided him. "The United States Surgeon General says smoking can be hazardous to your health."

Murphy took a long drag. "Word gets around, doesn't it?" He considered dropping the smoke to the pavement and stomping it out with his boot. Instead, he took another drag. "I'm trying to cut back."

Romana began her story.

The year before she came to Stockholm as part of a delega-tion from Eritrea trying to obtain humanitarian aid from Swedish charities.

"Most people in Eritrea have little access to doctors or medicines and we want to change that," she explained. "In the past, the Swedish people have provided assistance. They helped build a hospital in Asmara. But we want them to help the people in the little towns and small villages far away from Asmara."

Murphy had firsthand knowledge of who controlled most of the countryside in Eritrea, a rebellious province in Ethiopia.

"So you are working with the rebels?"

Romana remained silent.

"But I thought you were an American citizen," Murphy contin-ued. "Won't you get into trouble for helping the rebels?"

Romana grew sullen.

"The U.S. government doesn't care what I do," she said. "In its eyes, I'm not an American citizen. I don't have any papers. My father died before I was born, and there is no official proof I am an American."

When they first met, Romana told Murphy her father was among a contingent of American workers who came to Ethiopia to do salvage work after the Italians had scuttled their Red Sea fleet in the harbor at Massawa early during World War II.

After they met, Murphy wondered whether Smyth, the man from the American consulate in Asmara who helped him during his brief visit to Ethiopia, could help Romana. He doubted it. Handling requests for United States citizenship probably wasn't in his line of work.

"I thought you stayed in touch with your father's family in Maine," Murphy said. "I thought they considered you part of their family."

"Yes, the Alleys have accepted me as one of their own, but the U.S. government hasn't." The bitterness in Romana's voice remained. "So I will remain an Eritrean, and I will help my people win their freedom."

Romana told Murphy how much Asmara had changed since he was there.

"It's not the same place," she said. "The police are everywhere. They watch everyone."

Murphy knew Romana wasn't prone to exaggeration. She had always told him exactly what was happening.

Murphy recalled his own experience with the ubiquitous mufti-clad Ethiopian national police during his visit to Kagnew Station. How he was marched through downtown Asmara at gunpoint. How he was grilled by an Ethiopian police inspector at Centrale, the main police station in Asmara.

No, Romana wasn't exaggerating. Murphy was sure.

Romana said a few of her friends had left the city to join the rebels in the Eritrean countryside. After they left Asmara, she was sure the police began watching her.

"They even opened my mail and stole from me," she said. "One time, my father's family sent me a package from Maine, presents for my birthday. When it arrived, the box was empty."

"Can you tell me what you do here?" Murphy asked.

When it came to Murphy, Romana seldom had secrets. Apparently, that hadn't changed. Or had it?

"I translate, mostly," she said. "I've been learning Svenska since the day I arrived. I speak it pretty well."

Murphy was aware of Romana's facility with languages. She already spoke English, Italian and Tingrinya, her native tongue, well, and she had a smattering of Amharic, the primary language in Ethiopia. Now, she had picked up Svenska, too

Romana began to apologize again.

"I'm sorry you had to listen to all my problems," she said. "I'm sure you have more important things to do. I didn't mean to distract you from what you were doing."

"I wish there was something I could do for you," Romana continued. "Some way, I can help you."

"Help me?" Murphy murmured. "I don't think there's much you can do to help me, right now."

GUNDERSON LED Lund over the stone bridge along Riks-gatan, the broad passageway running between the two massive pink-hued neoclassical-designed buildings that made up Parliament House.

As the two policemen walked through the ornate archway at the end of Riksgatan, the north facade of the royal palace, which loomed on a hill above Parliament House, came into view.

After walking across the small square in front of the old mint, the two policemen trod up the long set of stone steps that ran up the hill next to the red-bricked palace. Nearing the entrance of the palace's outer courtyard, they heard band music blaring from within. The two men stopped and peered into the large parade ground inside the courtyard, where two groups of blue-clad soldiers stood at attention.

"The changing of the palace guard," Gunderson muttered. "Big deal."

Several hundred people, primarily families and elderly couples, stood behind rope barriers watching the daily ritual as the rays of the noon sun glistened off the musicians' instruments and the helmets of the soldiers.

"It's good for the tourists," Lund explained. "It's something for them to see."

Lund and Gunderson moved on, walking toward the old stock exchange building, where the large group of peace protesters milled around the stone obelisk in the cobblestone square.

The large red banner had been unfurled at the base of the monument. Their rhythmic chants competed with the martial music emanating from the courtyard.

"Hippies," Gunderson muttered as he walked next to Lund.

130

"*Fred och Karlek!*" He flashed the police inspector a two-fingered peace sign.

"It sounds better in English," Lund said. "Peace and Love."

Gunderson's English was not very good. He repeated the phrase with a distinctly Swedish twist. "Piss and Louvre."

"Peace and Love," Lund repeated. Then, in Svenska, he said: "Very well spoken, Officer Gunderson. We'll make a linguist out of you yet."

The police inspector suppressed a chuckle.

The two policemen avoided the crowd of people in the square and walked down Kallargrand toward the square in front of the Swedish Academy.

Gunderson took another look at the slip of paper Miss Waldman had given them. "The man we are looking for lives just down there." He pointed toward one of the narrow streets radiating from the square.

"You seem to know your way around here," the police inspector observed.

Gunderson smiled. "A friend of mine—he's a cop, too—lives in Södermalm." The young policeman gestured toward the direction they were headed. "We used to come here to chase girls. Sometimes, I caught one. When I was younger, I spent a lot of time here, Max."

The remark amused Lund. "When you were younger, you say? You sound like an old man looking back at his youth near the end of his life. You're still a young man. Judging from the way you eyed Miss Waldman, I can see you're not done chasing women."

"It was that obvious?" Gunderson asked.

Lund nodded. "There's nothing wrong with giving a woman an appraising look. I still do it."

"Really?" Gunderson said. "You still look at other women. But you're married, Max."

"Just because I'm married doesn't mean I'm blind," Lund explained. "Perhaps I'm just a bit more subtle in my appraisals now."

Except for a couple huddled together on a bench near the memorial, the square was empty.

As the two policemen strolled past the weathered stone memorial, the smell of a cigarette wafted through the air.

"He has expensive tastes," Gunderson remarked, sniffing the air. "Smells like a Rothman." He looked back at the source of the smoke. "And he's accompanied by a negress."

Lund followed the young policeman's gaze.

"He looks like a bum," the police inspector said. "Probably, visitors from America."

They walked on.

It took the two policemen about ten minutes to walk from the bridge to the address Miss Waldman had given them.

Lund and Gunderson knocked on a door just inside of the downstairs foyer in the small apartment building.

An elderly woman answered. She directed them to a flat on the second floor. "He's up there," she croaked. "With all the other Americans."

When Lund's next knock was answered, he was greeted by a tall, thin red-headed man wearing an apron much too small for him and holding a large wooden spoon in one hand.

The police inspector spoke in English. "Are you Reverend Frederick Burgess?" Lund held up his police credentials.

"Yes, that's who I am." Burgess seemed perplexed. "What do you want? How can I help you?"

For a moment, no one spoke. Finally, Lund broke the awkward silence. Again, he spoke in English. "I'm sorry for the intrusion," he apologized. "But your help is needed in a matter confronting the police. May we enter?"

"By all means." Burgess, still wearing a puzzled look, stepped aside so the two policemen could walk past him into the apartment. *"Hej."*

Lund returned the greeting in English. "Hello." As the police inspector moved past the tall American minister, he asked: "Do you speak Svenska?"

"I'm afraid my Swedish is not good." Burgess sounded truly apologetic. "I've been here not quite a year, and most of the people I deal with speak very good English, so I have been slow to learn your language. But I'm trying to improve."

"No problem," Lund said. He followed Burgess into the kitchen. "My English is pretty good. My wife is a language teacher, and we speak English when we are at home."

Burgess offered the two policemen chairs at the small Formica table next to the wall across the kitchenette from the gas stove on which a large metal pot sat bubbling away. Wisps of steam curled to the low ceiling.

Before he sat down, Lund spoke to Gunderson in Svenska.

"I have to speak to the American in English because he doesn't understand our language well," he told the young patrolman. "Stand by for awhile. And keep quiet."

When he turned his attention back to Burgess, Lund reverted back to English. "I'm sorry for speaking Svenska in front of you," he apologized again. "It is bad manners. Officer Gunderson, my associate, doesn't speak English well, and I wanted to explain the situation to him."

At that moment, hot water began gushing from the top of the large pot. Burgess moved across the room in one long step as it spilled onto the range. He slid the pot off the burner and lowered the heat. A few moments later, he put the pot back on the burner and began stirring its contents.

The room smelled of boiled onions and the savory scent of spices.

"The weather is rather humid to be cooking a stew," Lund observed.

It was quite warm in the little apartment. While toiling over the pot, Burgess' red hair had become matted. His face was flushed. Little rivulets of sweat cascaded from his pores.

"I agree," the young minister said.

Gunderson knew enough English to understand what Lund had just said. "Crazy Americans," he muttered. In Svenska.

The police inspector shot his young associate a sharp look but said nothing to him.

Burgess stood at the range with his back to the two policemen, unaware of the exchange.

"It's venison," he explained. Burgess kept stirring the pot. "A friend of mine shot a deer and gave me some meat. I have no way to store it. I must cook it or lose it."

"I understand," Lund said, shooting another glance in Gunderson's direction.

The young patrolman resumed his silent vigil.

The kitchenette was in the middle of the flat's three small rooms.

Gunderson took up a position against the wall behind Lund. From there, he could look through open doors into the other two rooms—the small living room overlooking the narrow street and the small windowless bedroom in the opposite direction at the rear of the apartment.

After a few moments, the stew resumed its contented bubbling, and Burgess returned to the chair across the table from Lund.

"Now, how can I help you?" the young minister asked.

The police inspector removed the composite from his briefcase and set it on the table in front of Burgess.

"We are seeking information about this man," Lund explained.

"We don't know his identity, and we want to talk to people who might have known him."

As the young minister studied the drawing, the police inspector described how a body was found floating in the Göta Canal. Lund told Burgess about the Globe and Anchor tattoo. He listed the dead man's height. His weight. Age. All approximates. He told Burgess of the date of his death. Another approximate. He revealed almost everything he knew about the dead man to the young American minister. Almost.

The one detail Lund left out was the fact the man pictured in the composite drawing was a murder victim. He didn't tell Burgess how the man in the canal had died.

After few moments of study, the young minister shook his head. "I'm sorry," he said. "I can't help you. I've never seen this man before."

The police inspector pushed the composite a little closer to Burgess. "Please take your time," he said. "The picture may not look exactly like the man we found. But we believe it's a good likeness."

Burgess studied the composite for a few more moments before coming to the same conclusion. "I'm sure." He pushed the picture back across the table toward Lund. "His face doesn't ring a bell. If I had seen him before, I would remember. He has quite distinctive features."

Lund understood. "The mouth?"

"Yes, the lip," Burgess nodded. "None of the military protesters I've met have a harelip."

"And you know all of the military protesters, as you call them?"

"Oh no, not all of them," Burgess answered. "As I told you I've been in Sweden for almost a year. During that time, I've met maybe two, three hundred of the men who have come here to protest their military service. There are hundreds I haven't met.

They live all over Sweden, not just in Stockholm."

At that moment, Lund recognized the scope of his problem. This investigation wasn't going to be easy. He was going to have to change his tack. He didn't have time to go door-to-door with the composite drawing searching for the identity of a dead man.

"Perhaps there's a place where some of these American military protesters congregate," the police inspector thought out loud. "Maybe you know of such a place. A club, perhaps."

Before Burgess could answer, Gunderson interrupted.

In Svenska, he told Lund: "Others are staying in this apartment."

In English, the police inspector apologized for the intrusion. "Excuse me for a moment, Reverend Burgess, but I must speak to my young associate. Apparently, he has something to tell me that can't wait."

Then Lund switched to Svenska. "What is it this time?"

Gunderson shared his discovery. "There are others who are living here, Max," he told the inspector. "I can see the couch in the front room has been slept on, and there are two beds in the back room. Maybe, whoever is sleeping here knows the identity of the dead man."

"Perhaps, your English is better than I thought," Lund observed. "You understood what I've been talking to this young American about."

Gunderson, wearing a boyish grin, nodded. "*Ja.*"

Returning his attention to Burgess, Lund deftly reverted back to English. "Officer Gunderson says you have guests staying with you."

The police inspector glanced back over his shoulder toward the room behind him. "Is someone staying with you?"

Burgess nodded.

"Who are they?"

Reverend Fred told Lund about the arrival the day before of Conrad and Murphy on the auto ferry from West Germany. Burgess held nothing back. He filled in the police inspector on the backgrounds of both men. Or at least as much as he knew about them.

"So Conrad, who is the younger of the two, is an American soldier who has come to Sweden to live, and Murphy is a tourist who is traveling on the cheap." Lund summed up what he'd been told. "Is that it?"

"In a nutshell, Inspector Lund."

"A nutshell, huh?" He smiled across the table at Burgess. "That's a new one for me. A nutshell. I like that."

Lund stood up from the table. "I want to look at the bedroom. Is that all right?"

Burgess shrugged. "I guess so." The young minister seemed unsure of his rights, whether he could prevent the Swedish police from conducting a search in his apartment. "I don't see why not."

In Svenska, Lund told Gunderson to proceed into the back room.

In English, the police inspector said to the young minister: "After you." Then he trailed Gunderson and Burgess into the bedroom.

As he entered the room, Gunderson immediately noticed Murphy's backpack on one of the bunks. In Svenska, the young patrolman asked Lund: "Shall I look?" He pointed at the canvas bag under the cot.

The police inspector nodded.

After pawing through the contents of the backpack for a few moments, the young police officer extracted Murphy's passport. Before resuming his search, he handed the thin booklet to Lund.

The police inspector thumbed through the pages of the travel document.

"This fellow has been around," he said in English. "In Greece and Ethiopia, three years ago. Two years ago, Panama. A week ago, Belgium. Then the Netherlands. West Germany. And the day before yesterday, he comes to Sweden. Through Trelleborg."

Lund handed the passport back to Gunderson. "Put it back where you found it," he told him in Svenska. "Try to make it look like nothing was disturbed. We don't want our American guests to think we're a bunch of snoops."

Then, in English, Lund told Burgess. "I'm sure everything is as you say it is." He glanced toward Gunderson, who was hovering over one of the cots trying to rearrange the contents in the backpack in the manner in which he found them. "I'm sorry about the intrusion."

As the three men walked back into the kitchenette, Lund recalled the question he had asked the young minister before Gunderson made his discovery. "I was asking you if there were places where the Americans tend to congregate."

Burgess nodded.

"There is such a place. Right around the corner up the street."

CRIES OF "*Selam*" greeted Murphy and Romana as they entered her apartment, located on one of the narrow alleys radiating from the square in the front of the Swedish Academy.

Romana handled the translation. "They are saying 'hello' to you."

In response, the CID investigator smiled, mouthed an awkward "*Selam*," followed by a quick "hello."

Romana introduced Murphy to the two sisters, Zula and Senait. Earlier, Zula, the younger of the pair, had bade Murphy "bye-bye." Apparently, that was all the English either of the girls knew. Romana translated as the two young Eritreans exchanged pleasantries with Murphy.

During the brief walk to her flat, Romana told Murphy about the two young women. Still in their teens, they had come to Sweden to receive medical training. "Mostly, they're learning about first aid," she explained. "They're going to be here just for a little while. When they return to Eritrea, they will pass on what they've learned to other women."

Romana, who Murphy knew had trained in Italy to become a nurse, was their teacher. She said several teams of young Eritrean women had rotated through Sweden during the previous year taking nursing lessons from her.

Murphy was impressed. "That must keep you busy."

"For now, it is my life," Romana said. "Some day, I hope to return to Eritrea and help even more."

Zula and Senait were preparing lunch.

A pungent odor filled the apartment. It emanated from the stew Zula tended in a pot on the burner of a small gas stove in a corner of the kitchen, which also served as the living room of the two-room flat. On the other burner, *enjera*, the flat bread Murphy had sampled during his brief stay in Asmara three years before, slowly baked in a pan. On a sideboard, a stack of the sponge-like bread, thicker than a crepe but thinner than a pancake, stood cooling between two plates.

"Z*igne*?" Murphy asked

"Don't worry," Romana laughed. "It's not as hot as we make it back home. We can't get all the ingredients here in Sweden."

Murphy sniffed. "Smells pretty tangy to me."

Nearby, Senait knelt on the floor using a mortar and pestle to grind coffee beans. A small charcoal-fired brazier sat next to her on a little tripod. Smoke curled up toward a small open window, which vented it outside toward the front of the narrow three-story apartment building.

"Remember the last time I had *zigne*?" Murphy asked.

Romana thought for a moment. Then, she smiled. "The last time was the first time. Wasn't it? In the tent at the wedding party that night in Ghezabanda?"

Murphy nodded, then laughed. "You're right, the last time was the only time. That stuff was too hot for me."

Sendait finished brewing the coffee.

As Murphy and the women squatted on the floor around the small wicker table set in the middle of the room, Zula poured some of the stew from the pot onto a thick stack of *enjera*. Small chunks of beef and four boiled eggs floated on top of the thick mixture of vegetables and broth.

As the women tore into the *zigne*, Murphy hesitated. "Eat," Romana pleasantly ordered, gesturing as she held a thick wad of the bread between the thumb and forefinger of her right hand.

Murphy tore off a piece of the bread with his fingers, swept it through the stew and sopped up some liquid, vegetables and a small chunk of meat. After he stuffed the mixture into his mouth, he was pleasantly surprised. It was mild, quite unlike the fiery *zigne* he sampled in Asmara three years before.

"Not too bad," he mumbled, wiping the back of his hand across his mouth. "Not too bad at all."

And so the four of them slowly dined. As they ate, the two young women peppered Romana with questions, mostly about Murphy. Apparently. As in the past, Romana served as an intermediary. Patiently, she translated their questions into English for Murphy, then translated his answers into Tigrinya for Zula and Senait.

"They want to know if you are married."

Murphy looked at Romana. "They want to know if I'm married?"

"Yes." There was that familiar smile again. "That's what they want to know." Then, as Romana turned away, Murphy followed her gaze in the direction of the two young women. As they waited for his answer, each wore a quizzical expression.

"No." Murphy shook his head. "I'm not married."

Romana shared his answer with the two young women.

Apparently, Zula wanted to know more. After Romana finished her translation, the pretty young Eritrean woman asked another question.

This time, it took Romana a few seconds to compose the translation.

"What does she want to know now?" Murphy asked.

Before Romana completed the translation, she glanced in Zula's direction. Just for a second. Then she looked Murphy in the eye.

"She wants to know if you have a lover." Romana asked. "No, that's not quite right." She stopped for a second and glanced toward Zula one more time. "What she wants to know is if you have a girlfriend. That's what she wants to know."

Murphy told them about Kate. Romana translated. Then Murphy told them about Tommy, Kate's son. Romana translated. He didn't say anything more about the relationship.

As the two young women heard Murphy's story slowly unfold through Romana's translations, their friendly, excited expressions gradually were replaced with a different look.

It was one of concern. With each phrase Romana spoke to them in Tigrinya, both glanced in their tutor's direction. It was as if they were wondering how she was reacting to Murphy's revelations.

Murphy began to share the same concern.

Romana gave no clue to her reaction to hearing the details of the CID investigator's life since the two had last seen each other. She just did her job. She translated the information she was receiving in English into Tigrinya.

After a while, the young women's interest in Murphy waned. They had heard enough. Apparently, they had learned what they wanted to know.

The conversation went on just between Murphy and Romana, as their two young dining companions remained respectfully silent.

"How's your mother?" Murphy asked. He remembered how she had predicted a dire future for him while reading a deck of playing cards during his visit to Ethiopia. "She still telling fortunes?"

Romana's answer was terse. "She died."

Murphy stopped eating. "Oh." He was genuinely saddened. He had liked Romana's mother. "I'm sorry to hear that. What happened?"

Romana grew serious. "She died of a fever during the winter more than a year after you left. She caught a chill, and it got worse. Then, she was gone."

"You must miss her."

Romana mustered an ironic little smile. "Yes, I do." Then, she grew thoughtful. "If she was still alive, maybe things would be different for me. Maybe, we would have gone to Italy. Or maybe, even the United States. Who knows?"

The CID investigator changed the subject.

"What about your old friend, Mekele?" He was an Eritrean rebel Murphy had encountered during his brief stay in Asmara. "Still up to his old tricks?"

Romana's mood brightened a bit. "Mekele. Now, there's a name from the past." She smiled at Murphy. "I don't see him, but I hear a lot about him. He's still fighting against the government. He's one of our leaders."

Murphy grew quiet. He lit a cigarette. He thought about Romana's mother. About Mekele. And about what Romana was doing in Sweden.

Then Murphy thought about Mouse. And about Andrews, the murderer he was trying to find.

Murphy decided it would be unwise to involve Romana in what he was doing in Sweden. He should keep his distance from her. He could mean trouble for her. It could make it impossible for her to stay.

Romana's plate was quite full. Murphy didn't want to add to it.

Not long after they finished eating, Murphy got up to leave.

"I've got to go," he said. "Before I go back to the states, I'll try to see you again. But I can't guarantee it."

"I understand," Romana said as she walked Murphy to her door.

"Good luck with your search." Then, a final "*Selam.*"

BY THE TIME Inspector Lund and officer Gunderson arrived at the Den Roda Raven, the noontime crowd had thinned out.

Most of the booths were empty, and only a handful of people, scruffy-looking men mostly, sat drinking their lunch on the few stools lining the bar.

The two policemen received a cool reception.

As soon as Lund flashed his inspector's badge to the bartender, two men, the scruffiest-looking of the bunch, got up and walked out the door, leaving their half-drained bottles of lager sitting on the wooden countertop.

Lund's eyes followed the two men as they walked past him, but neither one of them returned his stare.

"What the hell do you guys want?" the bartender sputtered. "You're driving my customers away. You're not the local fuzz."

Before Lund could explain the purpose of their visit, Gunderson intervened.

"Fuzz?" The young policeman sounded incredulous. "You have been watching too much American television. Perhaps you should show a little more respect for the badge."

The barman grunted. "Maybe so." Then, he reached under the bar and turned up the audio on the tape deck piping music into the tavern.

Immediately, the unremitting clang of Corey Laing's cowbell followed by the overpowering voice of Leslie West straining to belt out the opening lines of "Mississippi Queen" flooded into the room.

"What is that shit?" Gunderson asked.

"*Mountain,*" the barman answered, trying to bob his bald head in time to the beat. "American rock. A lot of my customers like it."

Gunderson didn't. "Turn it down," he snapped.

Ignoring the order, the barman smiled back at the young policeman. "It's a free country, isn't it?" He didn't expect an answer to his question.

Lund tacitly agreed with Gunderson's assessment of the music blaring over the sound system. When it came to American music, the police inspector tended toward Perry Como or Tony Bennett. But he also had to agree with the barman. Sweden was a free country.

Lund took control. Placing a restraining hand on the right arm of his young colleague, he said: "Please turn the music down." It was a request, not an order, spoken in a calm voice just loud enough to be heard above the din. "We want to talk to you about some of your customers."

The barman nodded, "Okay." The music was muted, and West's wail receded into the background. "What do you want to know about my customers?"

Lund placed his briefcase on the countertop and removed the composite. Holding it up for the bartender to view, he asked: "Do you recognize this man?"

The barman glanced at the picture for a few seconds before responding curtly: "Never seen him before."

"Are you sure?" Gunderson asked. "Take a good look."

"I'm positive," the barman said. "With a puss like that, it would be difficult to forget that man."

Lund agreed. The composite drawing did accentuate the major component of the dead man's facial features. His harelip. As drawn, such a face would be difficult to forget.

"We believe he was an American," the police inspector said. "We understand a lot of Americans come into your bar."

The barman smiled. "They like the music and they like the little foxes."

Lund got the distinct impression the barkeeper wasn't refer-
ring to the dozen or so pictures of the sleek, bushy-tailed animal
hanging on the pub's walls. No. He was talking about a different
kind of fox.

"Dozens of Americans come in here all the time. I see those
fellows nearly every day," the barman continued. "Then, there
are the ones who come in maybe once or twice with Reverend
Fred."

The entire interview with the barman was conducted in
Svenska. However, when he referred to the young minister who
worked with the American military deserters, he lapsed into English. It was "Reverend Fred."

During the past several months, the barman said, Burgess
had brought dozens of Americans into his bar. "I see their faces
only once or twice and I forget them." The barman took another
look at the composite drawing. "But I know the man in the picture is not one of my regulars. I would tell you if he was."

Lund looked around the near-empty bar. "Any of your American regulars here now?"

The barman looked around the room. "No," he said. "It's too
early. Most of them are working now. They can't stay in Sweden
unless they work or go to school. A few of them will come in
here later."

It was becoming clear to Lund the visit to the Den Roda Raven had been a waste of time.

In fact, the police inspector was starting to think the trip to
Stockholm had been a waste. The visit with Miss Waldman
hadn't produced any results. Yet. And it looked like the inter-
views with Burgess and now the barman of Den Roda Raven
had been as fruitless.

It occurred to Lund he might as well have spent the day
back in Mariestad working on some of the other cases that had

reached his desk, rather than follow one dead end after another in Stockholm.

Abruptly, the police inspector ended the interview. "I want to thank you for your time," he told the barman. "You have been very helpful."

As the two policemen turned to leave, the barman held up the two copies of the composite Lund had left on the counter-top. "What do I do with these?" he asked, waving the pictures at Lund and Gunderson.

"Show them to your customers," Lund suggested.

Gunderson offered another suggestion. "Hang one up over your pisser so your customers can study it while they pass your beer."

Lund shot the young police officer a reproachful look.

"Just show the picture to your customers," Lund repeated. "If any of them recognize the man in the picture, call the telephone number on the circular."

THE SKIES were leaden, but it remained light out when Gunderson dropped Inspector Lund off at his cottage in Karlsvik.

Only his wife, Marta, was at home to greet him.

The Nillsons' Volvo was gone.

"Where are Anita and Peter and the children?" Lund asked.

"In town at the Theatro," his wife answered. "The chamber players from Toreboda are playing Schubert."

"I like Schubert," Lund smiled. "Harmonious. Melodic. Just right for a summer evening." Then he looked at the gray clouds above. "Although it looks like rain tonight."

Despite the threatening skies, the Lunds sat out on the small deck in front of their cottage.

"How was your trip?" Marta asked.

Lund stopped smiling. "Not very productive, I'm afraid."

As he reviewed his trip to Stockholm, the police inspector showed his wife the circular.

"Funny," she said, after carefully studying the drawing. "He doesn't look Swedish."

"He's not," Lund said. "We think he's an American." He told his wife about the tattoo, the Globe and Anchor, and its connection with the United States Marine Corps. "The trouble is no one seems to know who he is, or how he came to be in Sweden."

Lund grew silent. In his mind, he again went over the trip to Stockholm and how little he gained from it. Maybe it was time to pull the plug and turn the case over to someone else. His wife suddenly ended his revelries.

"Oh, Magnus, there was a call for you today," Marta said.

"A call?" Lund perked up. "About the case?"

His wife shook her head. "No, nobody from the department

called, but Superintendent Persson from Gothenburg was looking for you."

Persson? Lund rarely spoke to the man. "What did he want?"

"He wanted to know where you were," Marta stated.

"And you said?"

"I told him I didn't know where you were," she explained. "I
said I thought you were out in the field somewhere, working on
a case. I told him you rarely share information with me when
you're working on a case. It's police business."

Lund smiled. "Good girl. That was a good answer."

Marta returned his smile with a satisfied grin. "He seemed to
like my explanation."

But there was more. Marta went on to explain the real reason
for the police superintendent's call. "He wanted to know when
you were going to finish moving your files into your new office.
The superintendent said you need to move your things out tomorrow. He said you will be the last to leave."

Lund was supposed to have devoted some of his time during
the past few days sifting through his records, discarding files he
no longer needed before moving into the new police station. It
was another headache that wouldn't go away.

Marta had one more piece of information to share with her
husband, but it required the couple to take a walk down to the
narrow cove, where there was a little beach, a sandy break in
the rocky shoreline, shared by all the residents of Karlsvik.

There, Marta showed Lund the little dinghy. It had been
beached with its hull up. Towards the stern, a fist-sized hole had
been punched through the plywood well below the water line.

"What happened?" Lund asked.

"The wind shifted, and it got a little rough out in the bay,
so Arvid and Britta tried to put in at the cove," Marta said.
"When they did, the waves carried them onto the rocks along

the shore, and they poked the hole in the boat."

Usually, Torso, the large island to the northwest, protected the bay from the heavy seas coming off Lake Vänern. But sometimes, when the breeze shifted from the northeast, the wind was funneled down the east side of the island and whipped across the kilometer-long causeway connecting it with the mainland.

"Are they all right?" Lund asked.

"They're fine." Marta nodded. "They're a couple of old salts. Just got a little wet."

Lund inspected the hole more closely. Carefully breaking off the tiny wooden fibers to avoid getting a splinter, he tried to get a better idea of the size of the breach. "Old salts? What do you mean?"

Marta chuckled. "Another bit of American slang. It means they are experienced sailors. They knew what they were doing. They had an adventure."

The couple began to walk along the dirt road back to their cottage.

"Peter said he can fix the dinghy," Marta went on. "He said he will put a fiberglass patch on before he leaves." Then, she added: "He spent most of the day working on our sauna. He got a lot done."

As soon as they got back to the cottage, Lund inspected his brother-in-law's handiwork. Nillson had attached the outside sheathing to the frame, installed the door and had even shingled the roof.

"Peter was a busy boy," Lund told his wife.

"Tomorrow, he plans to finish the wiring," Marta said.

The police inspector was impressed.

His brother-in-law had a plan how to proceed with the construction of the sauna.

Lund really didn't have a clue about the next step he would take in his project.

DON COULTER CAUGHT an early train from the central station in downtown Stockholm and arrived in Laxa before noon. Mouse, as he was called by everybody who knew him, had a lot to tell Marlon Andrews.

On the five-hour train trip, which included a transfer to a southbound passenger train in Orebro, Coulter had settled on a priority list.

First, Mouse would tell Fish about how someone had apparently searched his room while he was out making his rounds two days before.

Next, he would show him the flyer the police were circulating in an effort to learn the identity of the dead man found in the Göta Canal.

Mouse knew who the dead man was. He also knew how the body got into the canal, and so did Andrews. Now the police had recovered it.

When the train reached Laxa, Coulter was the only passenger to get off. The station master, a little man with a droopy mustache and bushy eyebrows, waved to him as the drug dealer began to trudge down the well-worn path to the trestle that carried the highway over the tracks.

It took him nearly thirty minutes to walk out to the commune.

Andrews was sitting at a table in the main room of his cabin with a pair of scissors in his hand. Coulter caught him by surprise.

"What the fuck are you doing here? You weren't due for another two, three days."

Fish was in his usual mood.

151

"We got problems," Mouse stammered. "We got some big problems."

Andrews put down the scissors and pushed the piece of paper he had been working on off to the side. Then he stood up, sidled up to Mouse, placed a firm hand on his shoulder and guided him back out the door.

"Let's go out and sit in the sun," he said, "and you can tell me all about our problems."

As he was propelled out the screen door, Mouse looked toward the main house. It looked deserted.

"Where are Jhonas and the others?" he asked.

Andrews shrugged. "They went down south to a music festival. Be back in three, four days."

After the two men sat down at the table near the mill pond, Coulter began to spin his tale.

First, just as he planned it, Mouse told Andrews he was sure someone had been in his room while he was out selling drugs.

"What makes you think that?" Andrews sounded skeptical.

"Izzy told me."

"Who the hell is Izzy?"

Before Mouse responded, he paused to collect his thoughts. He knew Fish wasn't going to like his answer.

"Her name is Isabelle," he said. "She's my girlfriend."

Andrews exploded. "Girlfriend? What did I tell you about girlfriends?"

Mouse sounded contrite. "I know. You told me not to get involved with anybody. Keep a low profile and do my job is what you told me. I screwed up, but it's a good thing I did."

Andrews calmed down. "How so?"

Mouse told him how his girlfriend came looking for him a couple of days before and found his door unlocked.

Andrews wasn't impressed. "So?"

Mouse explained. "The thing is I wasn't there. I was out when Izzy dropped by and I had hooked the padlock on the outside of the door when I left."

Andrews was intrigued. "So you're saying someone sprung the lock and went inside."

Mouse nodded.

"They take anything?"

Mouse shook his head. "No, everything was like I left it. Nothing was missing."

Andrews rubbed his beard. "Well, that is a problem."

Coulter hoisted his backpack onto the table and reached inside. "And look at this," he said, removing the flyer he had taken from the Den Roda Raven the night before.

Andrews's look turned grave. "So they found Sully, huh?"

Coulter nodded.

Andrews studied the flyer for a few moments. "Where did you get it?"

"I took it off the wall in the Red Fox Den in the Old Town," Mouse responded.

"Anybody see you take it?"

Mouse shook his head. "It was hanging over the toilet in the head," he explained. "I was all by myself."

Andrews resumed rubbing his beard. "And then you left the first thing this morning?"

Coulter nodded.

"And nobody followed you to the train station?"

Coulter shook his head. "I don't think so."

Andrews seemed perturbed. "You don't think so, huh?"

Mouse knew Andrews was unhappy with him.

"What did I tell you to do if something like this happened?"

Coulter knew the right answer to that question. "You told me to stay away."

Andrews cracked a slight grin. "Aaah, the light bulb goes on."

Andrews stood up and looked out at the millpond for a few moments before turning back to face Coulter. "What if you were followed? What if someone tailed you here?" He gestured toward the main road on the other side of the pond. "What if the cops were coming down the road, right now?"

Mouse tried his best to reassure Andrews. "Fish, I'm pretty sure I wasn't followed." He tried to sound confident. "I did what I usually do, I bought a through ticket to Gothenburg, but I'm positive I was the only one to get off the train here."

Andrews sat down. He looked out over the pond, rubbing his beard, apparently lost in thought.

Mouse grew fidgety. He didn't like it when Andrews went silent on him.

"What are we going to do, Fish?" It was a plea. "Do you have a plan?"

After a few more moments of silence, Andrews returned his gaze to Coulter.

"Yeah, I think I got a plan," he said. "I think I got a plan that will take care of all of our problems."

MURPHY'S MORNING began with his discovery that Mouse had pulled up stakes and left town.

The little drug dealer had cleared out. His padlock was gone. His backpack was gone. His drug stash was gone. His room was empty.

Murphy went through the room from top to bottom twice to see whether Mouse had left anything behind. He flipped the mattress. He inspected every nook and cranny in the interior of the wooden wardrobe. He got down on his hands and knees and groped under the armoire. He picked up the water pitcher on the small dry sink and held it upside down. He wedged his way under the bed springs for a closer look. He found nothing.

When he was done, Murphy sat down on the side of the bed and lit a cigarette, wondering what to do next.

Murphy knew he had lost a good lead.

At first, he considered just hanging around Gamla Stan until Mouse turned up again. But his experience working the streets of Philadelphia and New York told him there was no guarantee Mouse would return. No. He had to find another way to pick up his trail.

Abruptly, Murphy stood up and grabbed hold of the light fixture dangling from the coaxial cable hanging from the ceiling. Using it as a searchlight, he aimed the beam toward the dark recess in the corner of the room nearest the door. Slowly, he played the beam along the narrow baseboard of the wall facing him.

In the far corner, in the narrow gap between the wardrobe and the wall, the spotlight illuminated a small object.

Murphy got back down on his knees and reached into the gap.

It was a matchbook.

Standing under the naked light bulb, the CID investigator studied his find. It was like the other matchbooks he'd seen during his previous search of the little drug dealer's room. Its cover, both front and back, was decorated with a Red, White and Green replica of the Italian flag. There was no script.

This time, Murphy opened the matchbook to discover lettering inside the front cover.

From top to bottom, it read:

Valhommen till!

Cafe Romeo

Laxa, Orebro, Postgatan 5

Murphy concluded the matchbook was an advertisement for a restaurant. It was plain to see Mouse had spent some time there. He had felt comfortable enough in the place to help himself to several books of matches. Maybe a waiter or a waitress or someone who worked at the restaurant would be able to tell Murphy something about him. The CID investigator didn't know where the Cafe Romeo was, but maybe he knew someone who did.

It took Murphy less than five minutes to walk back to Reverend Fred's apartment. He found the tall lanky minister hunched over the kitchen table dipping a spoon into his morning bowl of Cheerios.

Murphy hadn't eaten breakfast yet, and Burgess knew it.

Pointing at the large yellow box of cereal with his spoon, he said: "Help yourself."

Both men knew they looked at the world quite differently on a number of levels, but at least they managed to remain cordial to one another.

Murphy was famished. After retrieving a bowl from the cupboard, he filled it nearly to the brim with the little OOOOOOs of oats. Then he splashed in some milk and dug in.

As they both sat crunching on the cereal, Reverend Fred told Murphy he had invited a group of war protesters over for dinner. He was going to serve them the stew he had started working on the day before. The kettle still sat simmering on his stove.

"You're welcome to join us, John."

Murphy really didn't want to spend an evening breaking bread with a group of military deserters, or war protesters as Burgess called them, but he needed a good reason for turning down the invitation.

He showed the matchbook to Reverend Fred.

"I like Italian food," Murphy said. "Thought I'd give it a try."

Burgess looked at the inside cover of the matchbook.

"Good luck," the young minister harrumphed. "You'd have to travel three hundred kilometers to give this restaurant a try. It's in Laxa."

Reverend Fred handed the matches back to Murphy.

"Where's Laxa?"

The minister dipped into his bowl for another spoonful of cereal. "It's in Orebro County, to the west, more than halfway to Gothenburg."

Murphy went silent momentarily, as he munched on his cereal.

"You been there?" he asked.

"Been where?" Burgess responded.

"To Laxa." Murphy tried to keep his interest in the matchbook conversational. He didn't went Burgess to think he was pushing for information. "I mean, how do you know about the place."

"I don't know anything about the restaurant," Burgess said. "But I do know something about the town. Used to be a mining town. Now they're trying to diversify. One of the boys got a job in a factory there before I got here. Then, he came back to Stockholm for another job placement. He said there was nothing to do in Laxa."

Murphy took one more look at the matchbook before he slipped it into the pocket of his jeans.

"It's too bad it's so far away and there's nothing to do there," he mused. "I really do like Italian food."

Burgess shrugged his shoulders.

"Well, I think Laxa is a little far to go for some pasta," the young minister said. "Maybe four, five hours west of Stockholm. It's in the sticks. In the woods."

As Murphy resumed eating his cereal, Burgess changed the subject.

He began talking about the visit from the two Swedish policemen. He showed Murphy the poster they had left him.

Murphy glanced at it. "Looks like he belongs on a post office wall," he said.

"Maybe so," Burgess said. "But they don't know who he is. His body was found in the Göta Canal, actually not far from Laxa, and they think he's an American."

Murphy took another look at the poster. For the first time, he noticed it was written in both English and Svenska. Height. Weight. Approximate age. It was all there. But there was no mention of nationality nor any indication of the cause of death.

Murphy handed the poster back to Burgess. "What makes them think he's an American?"

Using his empty spoon, Burgess pointed to his left shoulder. "Inspector Lund said he had a Globe and Anchor tattoo."

"I see," Murphy said. "He was a Marine."

Reverend Fred nodded as he munched on a mouthful of Cheerios.

Murphy resumed eating.

A few moments later, he put his spoon down.

"Did Inspector Lund say he would be coming back?" Murphy asked.

Burgess shrugged. "He didn't say."

Abruptly, Murphy got up from the table and walked down the hallway to the bedroom.

A few moments later, he stood in front of Reverend Fred with his backpack slung over his shoulder.

"Look," Murphy said. "I appreciate your hospitality, but I got to be shoving off. I don't tend to stay too long in any one place."

Reverend Fred nodded. "I understand."

Then, Burgess pointed to Murphy's knapsack. "By the way, one of the policemen looked through that while they were here. They looked at your passport."

"Did they say anything about it?"

The young minister smiled. "Only that you had been around."

Then Reverend Fred put his spoon down and extended his hand across the table. "Good luck," he said. "I hope you find what you are looking for."

Burgess had a surprisingly firm grip.

"Good luck to you, too, Reverend Fred," Murphy smiled. "I'm sure I'll find what I'm looking for. I usually do."

But Murphy knew he was going to need some help this time.

INSPECTOR LUND spent the morning moving boxes of records from his old office on Nygatan to the new police station up the road from the stately old Governor's Mansion.

Lund used the Saab to make the move, and it took more than one trip to transport the dozen or so cardboard boxes of material he had accumulated during his twenty years as a policeman.

By the time he had finished his breakfast, the police inspector had decided he would take the time to move the material now then go through it later after he had cleared the case he was working on.

After depositing his first carload of boxes in his new office, located in a wing of the new police station overlooking the high windowless east wall of the county lockup, Lund received his first break in the case.

The dispatcher told him the owner of the Den Roda Raven in Stockholm had called. He left his phone number.

The police inspector immediately returned the call.

The bar owner told him the composite drawing of the unidentified dead man had been removed from the bathroom wall. Then he told him who did it.

"Who did you say it was?" the police inspector asked.

Lund couldn't believe his ears.

"Mouse?" he responded. "Mouse? That's it."

The bar owner said Mouse was an American. He didn't know his real name, but he was able to provide the police inspector with a fairly complete physical description. He also told Lund he believed Mouse was selling drugs.

Before Lund made a second run to pick up more boxes from his old office, he conferred with Gunderson, who was hanging around the police station waiting to take the Dodge out on patrol. He wasn't the only member of the police force who liked to put The Rocket through its paces along the back roads in the rural areas surrounding Mariestad. Whoever drove the car always seemed to remain out on patrol longer than scheduled.

"Do you know anybody who works the drug scene in Stockholm?" Lund asked.

Gunderson nodded. "My friend, Bjorn, the one I told you about. He works undercover sometimes. Perhaps he can be of some assistance."

"Unofficially, right?" the police inspector cautioned.

The young patrolman nodded. "Of course."

Lund handed Gunderson the description the owner of the Den Roda Raven had given him. "He said he was an American and that his name was Mouse. He thinks he sold drugs."

Gunderson responded with a quizzical look.

"I know it is not much to go on," Lund conceded, "but maybe your friend from Södermalm can tell us a little bit more about this American drug dealer, this fellow called Mouse."

It took another trip with another load of boxes before Lund received his second break in the case.

This time, it was a call from a detective with the police department in Gothenburg. Finally, he was able to attach a name to the picture of the man on the flyer Lund had sent out. "His name is Paul Sullivan. He's an American."

The detective told Lund no one in his department had seen Sullivan for months. However, he said every cop in Gothenburg knew what the burly American with the harelip was up to. "He sold drugs," the detective said. "Small scale, mostly. Some marijuana. A little hash. LSD. Speed."

The detective said Sullivan would show up every few weeks for a few days to sell his small supply of drugs. "We figured he was working for someone else, and that was the guy we were really after, so we left him alone but we kept an eye on him."

"Did you get anywhere?" Lund interjected. "Did you find out who his boss was?"

"No." Lund could sense the dejection in the detective's voice. "No. We never were able to connect Sullivan with anyone locally."

But Lund sensed there was something else. He waited.

"But here's the strange part," the detective continued. "Every time he left town, he bought a ticket to Stockholm and took the train."

Nothing strange about that, Lund thought.

"The last time he left I had the police in Stockholm waiting to follow him when he got off the train there," the detective explained. "But he wasn't on that train. He'd gotten off somewhere between Gothenburg and Stockholm."

That was odd, Lund thought, not particularly helpful, but odd.

Lund had completed his third and final trip to retrieve boxes from his office in the old police station before he received yet another break in the case.

This time, it came when Gunderson briefed Lund about his conversation with his cop friend from Södermalm.

"Bjorn said he saw Mouse just today in Gamla Stan," the young patrolman reported. "Bjorn said he was following him around for the past three days, just keeping an eye on him."

Gunderson went on to tell Lund about his friend's assessment of Mouse. It sounded familiar. "Small-time stuff. Some marijuana. A little hash. A few hits of LSD and some speed."

"And where is this Mouse now?" Lund asked.

Gunderson shrugged. "Bjorn said he bugged out real early this morning. He bought a ticket on the early train to Gothenburg, but he never arrived. Bjorn called ahead to have someone pick up his trail when he got to Gothenburg, but he wasn't on the train. He got off some place in between."

"Strange," Lund began to think aloud. "An American drug dealer in Stockholm buys a train ticket for Gothenburg, but he never arrives there, and another American drug dealer in Go-thenburg buys a train ticket for Stockholm but he never arrives there."

Like most policemen, Lund didn't believe in coincidence.

"I wonder where they went?" he mused. "Wherever it is, I'm sure they ended up together."

Gunderson cleared his throat. He had something to add.

"There's more?" Lund asked.

"Bjorn said he wasn't the only one following Mouse," Gunder-son said.

"Is that so?"

Gunderson went on to provide the police inspector with a description of the man who was also tailing the American drug dealer.

"Bjorn said whoever he was, he acted like a professional," he said. "Real smart."

"Interesting," Lund commented.

BY THE TIME Murphy and Romana arrived at the little train station in Laxa it was mid-afternoon.

At first, Romana, despite offering to help just the day before, was reluctant to accompany Murphy.

"I don't want to get into trouble," she said.

What she meant was she didn't want to attract any attention.

"I'm here in Sweden legally for humanitarian reasons," she explained. "If the Swedish government learns I'm also training nurses to go back to Eritrea to help the rebels, it would cause problems. If they caught me helping you, they might kick me out."

Murphy was in the same boat. The CID investigator had to maintain a low profile, too. He was working undercover, and the Swedes could boot him out of the country if they found out what he was doing.

"Don't worry," he said. "No rough stuff, I promise. Nothing to attract attention. I just got to pin this guy down. Then I'll call somebody and they'll come and take away the trash."

Murphy had already told Romana about Marlon Andrews and how he murdered an American soldier in West Germany, and about Mouse and his drug stash.

Murphy handed her the matchbook.

"This is only the lead I got," he continued. "If I can pick up this guy's trail again, I know he'll lead me to where I want to go."

In the past, whenever Murphy followed his gut instincts, it worked.

Romana gave in, just a little. She told Murphy she would take him to Stockholm's central train station and put him on the right train.

But Murphy was adamant. He needed more help than that. In Ethiopia, it had been Romana's ability to speak her native Tingrinya and Italian and a smattering of Arabic that had helped him. Now, her fluency in Svenska is what he needed. Then Romana realized Murphy might have to change trains a couple of times during the trip inland. What if he got on the wrong train? How would he ask for directions? What if someone got suspicious about his desire to travel to Laxa, a little town located literally in the middle of nowhere, and decided to take a closer look at him? Romana didn't want to be the one responsible for getting her old friend in trouble. Finally, she talked herself into making the trip with Murphy.

"I'll go with you," she relented. "Someone needs to keep you out of trouble."

Murphy smiled. "I'll try to have you home by nightfall," he said. "Whenever that is. I promise."

It was a good time for Romana to slip out of town unnoticed. Her two nursing students, Zula and Senait, had already left for a cultural fair up north in the university town of Uppsala. They wouldn't return until the following afternoon. Hopefully, their tutor would be back in Stockholm by then.

During the first leg of their trip, a three-hour ride on a diesel-powered train to Orebro, the couple kept conversation to a minimum. Murphy didn't want anyone to overhear what Romana and he were talking about during the trip. Something might slip out.

"Loose lips sink ships," Van Dyck used to warn Murphy. Then, the old warrant officer would add. "It's a good thing we're in the Army, or we all would be treading water."

Murphy thought it best if it looked like he and Romana weren't even traveling together, so they sat in the coach on opposite sides of the aisle.

Before leaving Stockholm, Murphy bought a copy of the *International Herald Tribune* at a kiosk outside the central station. He paid four krona.

During the trip, Murphy alternated between reading the newspaper and staring out of the window at the Swedish countryside, while Romana practiced her Svenska with an elderly gentleman who sat in a seat facing her.

On the front page of the newspaper, Murphy read an analysis of the recent visit of Henry Kissinger, national security advisor to President Nixon, to the People's Republic of China. The columnist wondered whether it would lead to a change in the communist nation's relationship with the United States.

Murphy had his own ideas about the reasons for Kissinger's surprise visit to Red China. The President was trying to put the squeeze on the Russians and the North Vietnamese. From what Murphy could see during his two tours in South Vietnam, the Union of Soviet Socialist Republics was the primary supporter of the North Vietnamese in their effort to take over the South. The Chinese didn't like the Russians, and vice versa, and the Vietnamese had been fighting the Chinese for a thousand years. Nixon wanted to shake things up.

When Murphy looked out the window, the train skirted the north shore of a lake that reminded him of a lake in Maine he visited the previous summer during a camping trip with Kate and Tommy. Like in Maine, evergreens ran right down to the water's edge along the rocky shoreline, and the water, even from his seat in the comfortable SJ Pullman, looked cool and clear.

Another front page story caught Murphy's attention. It was a report on the attempted assassination of King Hassan II of Morocco. A group of military cadets, under the command of a couple of disgruntled senior officers, tried to stage a coup during a birthday party for the king at his summer palace in Rabat. Royalist troops attacked the palace and the king retained his throne. More than one hundred people were killed.

Murphy smiled. He knew Van Dyck would get a kick out of this story. "Never send a bunch of boys to do a man's job," he could hear the old warrant officer say.

This time, when Murphy paused his perusal of the newspaper to look out the window, a broad swath of pastureland ran from both sides of the track. The farmland was dotted with little red barns and silos.

In the distance toward the west, Murphy could make out the tree line where the forest began again. As the train grew closer, he noticed the trees spread out in a thick green carpet all the way to the horizon. Unlike in New England, where an occasional hardwood or an especially tall pine poked up through the canopy, these trees appeared to be of a uniform height, as if they'd been pruned to grow at the same rate.

On an inside page of the newspaper, Murphy read an article about Lee Trevino winning the 100th British Open at Royal Birkdale. The victory came less than a month after Trevino won his second U.S. Open title on the East Course of the Merion Golf Club in Ardmore, Pennsylvania.

Murphy knew it was quite an accomplishment for Trevino, who grew up learning to play the game on the public courses in Texas. Murphy learned to play the game on the historic old course at Harwich on Cape Cod, when he wasn't helping the superintendent groom the undulating greens or mow the narrow fairways.

At Orebro, the couple switched to a small electric-powered car for the short jaunt to Laxa. It was similar to the diesel-powered Littorina they rode on together in Ethiopia three years before, but it was roomier and much less crowded.

When they reached Laxa, Romana asked the station master

for directions to Postgatan. The short, bushy-browed man didn't say a word. He simply pointed out the front door of the little train station.

About a minute later, Murphy and Romana stood outside the Cafe Romeo looking at the menu hanging next to the entrance. The restaurant was closed. A sign indicated it would open and start serving dinner in about an hour.

Murphy couldn't wait. He rapped on the window next to the door.

Moments later, a dark-skinned teenager with a head full of black curly hair parted the curtain and peeked out the window. He pointed to the sign and yelled something in Svenska.

"He says they will open in about an hour," Romana translated.

Murphy thought quickly. "Tell him we don't want to eat now. Tell him we're looking for an American friend. Tell him our friend has dined here."

Romana delivered the message.

Moments later, the door opened, and the dark-skinned teenager peered out.

His name was Angelo. His father had come from Italy to open the restaurant about a decade before.

Romana switched to Italian, but Angelo said he no longer spoke his native tongue that well. They stuck to Svenska.

Murphy showed the matchbook to Angelo. "Tell him our friend gave this to me, and we've come to Laxa to visit him, but we don't know where he lives. Tell him his name is Mouse."

Angelo listened intently as Romana translated. His face seemed to light up when Romana mentioned the name "*Mus.*"

Angelo nodded. Pointing in the direction of the train station, he rattled off a torrent of Svenska. Murphy managed to pick out one word of his monologue. It was "hippies."

Instead of translating Angelo's long, apparently well-detailed answer, Romana summarized. "Angelo says Mouse lives about three or four kilometers north of town with a group of hippies. It's an easy walk, he says. He says you can't miss the place. It's a large cottage with two outbuildings lying on the far side of a millpond just off the main road. All the buildings are painted crimson. A little bridge from the main road runs over the narrow stream that feeds the pond, he says."

Murphy glanced toward Romana. "That was easy," he muttered. "Tell him perhaps we'll bring Mouse back for dinner."

Again, Romana delivered Murphy's message in Svenska.

As the couple turned to leave, Romana said "*Grazie*" to the young Italian-Swede.

Angelo smiled. "*Prego.*"

"At least he hasn't forgotten his Italian manners," Romana whispered.

Murphy and Romana followed the path next to the railroad tracks to the trestle. After climbing a steep incline, they reached the road to Karlskoga. After walking over the trestle, the couple immediately found themselves in the woods.

"We've done this before," Romana reminded Murphy.

Three years before, on the day they met, Murphy and Romana hiked up a steep hill from the Flats on the road that ran between Asmara and the Red Sea port of Massawa for a couple of hours before they hitched a ride to Asmara with an Arab trader and his driver.

"Yes, I remember," Murphy said, "but this is much different."

On this trip, Romana didn't wear high heels. Instead, she wore a pair of flats. This time, she didn't have to work as hard to keep up with Murphy's powerful strides.

It took them a little more than thirty minutes to trek out to the hippies' commune.

It was just as Angelo had described. An idyllic setting.

A large red cottage sat in the midst of two similarly-colored outbuildings in a sun-drenched clearing on the other side of the small mill pond running right up to the main road. A single steel plate, no more than five meters long and a little more than the width of a car in diameter, bridged a narrow stream.

The place looked deserted.

With Romana in tow, Murphy walked over the bridge for a closer inspection.

The doors to the two-story main house, both front and back, were locked.

Then Murphy checked the outbuildings, starting from behind the main house. While walking toward a long squat building in the rear, he noticed three pot plants growing in between the vegetable rows in the large garden on the other side of the house.

All the doors to the outbuilding, which looked like it could have been a stable at one time, were padlocked.

Next, Murphy and Romana checked out the cabin closest to the pond.

It was there they found the body.

IT TOOK two more telephone calls to prod Lund into action. The first came from Superintendent Persson, who wondered why the police inspector was spending so much time investigating an apparent suicide. Lund had never told his boss about the pathology report. It was his and Doctor Gustavson's little secret. "We just now have established his identity," Lund explained. Then, he fudged a bit more. "Now, we're trying to notify the family."

The superintendent indicated he knew more than he was letting on.

"His family?" Persson retorted. "I thought he was an American. You should call their embassy in Stockholm or inform the U.S. consulate in Gothenburg. Tell them who the dead man is. Dump the problem into their laps. The Americans can contact his family."

The superintendent seemed more concerned about Lund settling into his office space at the new police station. "Have you moved out yet?"

Lund assured his supervisor all of his files had been transported. "I was in the process of unpacking when you called, sir."

"Good," was all Persson said. Then, he abruptly rang off.

The phone rang again as Lund put the receiver back on its cradle.

It was Doctor Gustavson.

"Magnus," he said. "They are asking for the report at headquarters in Stockholm."

This caught Lund by surprise. "What? I thought I had three or four days."

The pathologist sounded apologetic. "I thought so, too," he

said. "But they apparently learned the dead man was an American, and they want me to expedite it."

Once Gustavson's supervisors saw that report, Lund knew he would no longer be allowed to work on the murder case. A team from the NCID would swoop in.

The police inspector needed just a little more time. "How long have I got? When will you send it?"

"It leaves by courier later this afternoon," Gustavson said. "My boss should see it first thing in the morning."

Lund had a little more time to work on it. "Basically, then, I must wrap up my investigation today," the police inspector summarized.

"Exactly," Gustavson replied.

By this time, Gunderson had taken The Rocket out on patrol. Lund asked the dispatcher to have him swing by the police station. "Tell him I need a ride."

A few minutes later, Gunderson brought the Polara to a screeching halt in front of the new police station, which looked more like a bank branch or an insurance agency with its large tinted plate glass windows and low-slung design.

The two policemen drove to the train station, located behind the cathedral and its leafy knoll about a kilometer down Nygatan from the old police station.

Lund intended to check the timetables for trains traveling between Gothenburg and Stockholm. He wanted to see whether there were common stops on the routes of trains traveling in both directions. It would give him an idea of just how difficult it would be track down the movements of the two drug dealers.

It turned out to be a good move.

The tall thin station master with bushy eyebrows and mustache was extremely helpful.

All Lund had to do was to show him the picture of Sullivan, the dead man.

"I've seen him before," the station master said.

"Where?"

"Here. He stopped here in Mariestad."

This was too good to be true, Lund thought. "How can you be so sure it was this man?" He glanced down at the flyer he held in hand.

The station master looked down at the flyer. "It's hard to forget a face like that," he said. "Besides, he stayed here for two hours to wait for a train. Nobody does that. Here, they get on the train. They get off the train. They don't hang around the station."

"Exactly when did this happen?" asked Lund.

The station master rubbed one of his furry eyebrows. "Must have been in March, just before the solstice," he answered. "He got off on the wrong stop on the train from Gothenburg. You know how dark it gets that time of year. He was confused."

Lund pressed for more information. "Where was he going?"

"Laxa," the station master said. "He was going to Laxa."

Interesting, thought Lund. But the police inspector needed the answer to one more question. "Tell me, do any of the trains going to Gothenburg from Stockholm stop at Laxa?"

After stepping to his desk, the station master flipped through several pages in his large book of timetables. "Yes, a train from Stockholm stops there three, no four times a day." He ran his finger further down and across the page. "Two times, they have to change trains in Orebro before they make that stop."

Lund and Gunderson headed north up the E3 highway to Laxa. Normally, it was a forty-five minute drive, but the young patrolman shaved ten minutes off the trip.

"Just use the lights," Lund requested when they got into The Rocket.

"I hate the klaxon."

Gunderson complied with Lund's request, and they still made the trip in record time.

The station master in Laxa looked oddly familiar. Although he stood much shorter, he had the same bushy eyebrows and mustache as the man Lund had talked to at the railroad station in Mariestad,

The police inspector commented on their physical similarities. "Oh, that's my brother Lars," said the station master. "Our father and our uncles all worked for the railroad. It's the family business. You know how it is."

Yes, Lund knew how it was.

The police inspector got down to business.

Lund showed the flyer to the station master. ""Have you seen this man before?"

The station master studied the picture for a few moments. Lund had seen this look before. Same furrowed brow. Same rubbing of his jaw with his hand.

Then came the answer.

"Yes, he used to come through here." The station master handed the flyer back to the police inspector. "I haven't seen him for a quite awhile though, maybe three or four months."

Lund folded the flyer and slid it back into the inside pocket of his jacket. "Did he live around here?" he asked.

The station master nodded. "I think he stayed with the hippies out in the commune," he gestured behind him toward the far side of the railroad tracks. "I think he spent a lot of time with the hippies."

"Hippies?" Lund asked. "There are American hippies here in Laxa?"

The station master chuckled. "No, not American hippies," he said. "Swedish hippies. They travel around going to festivals.

Regular gypsies."

"The family of their leader used to own most of the land around here. The kid doesn't have to work, so he doesn't."

Without any more prompting, the station master directed Lund to the location of the commune. After leading the two police outside the small red brick train station to the side of the railroad tracks, he pointed east in the direction of the trestle.

"It's three, four kilometers out on the main road to Karlskoga," he said. "Look for the mill pond to the right of the road. The hippies live in the large red cottage on the other side of the pond."

THE BODY LAY on its side on the small woven rug in front of the settee in the main room of the cabin.

Murphy knew who it was without turning the corpse onto its back. Mouse's left arm lay on the floor behind his head, and Murphy could see where the bullet had entered his torso right under his left armpit. Death was nearly instantaneous as there was just a small splatter of blood on the rug beneath the corpse.

"This guy never knew what hit him," Murphy said to Romana, who stood near the dead man's feet. "Pretty neat hit."

Murphy grabbed hold of the dead man's left wrist, lifted it and then let it drop. "This didn't happen too long ago," he said. "Rigor hasn't even set in." He glanced up at Romana. "You know what I mean?"

Romana nodded. "I'm a nurse, remember? I've seen my share of gunshot wounds, especially during my time with the liberation front."

Murphy stood up. "I got to take a look around."

While he conducted his search of the cabin, Murphy parked Romana in a spot in the small kitchenette, which was tucked into a corner near a doorway that led to two small bedrooms. "Don't move and don't touch anything," he told her. "I don't want to corrupt the crime scene."

Murphy moved quickly, but he made sure anything he disturbed was left as he found it. Working from the back of the cabin toward the front, he checked out the two bedrooms first but found nothing of interest.

Next, he tackled the main room.

On the small couch next to the body he found the small backpack he saw Mouse carrying in Stockholm. In it was the large paper bag Murphy had discovered taped to the underside of the armoire in Mouse's room. Aside from a dime bag of grass, two hits of LSD and a half-dozen matchbooks from Café Romeo, it was empty.

While looking in the drawer of the end table next to the settee, Murphy came across two American passports, a folded sheet of white paper, a pair of scissors and a small bottle of glue.

One of the passports belonged to Don Coulter, whose picture looked like a sad but spruced-up Mouse. "Well, at least we now know his name," said Murphy, sharing his discovery with Romana.

Murphy noticed the last entry stamp in the booklet was entered in Denmark. There was no exit stamp. "Looks like Mouse was in Sweden illegally," he said. "He never got a visa."

Then, Murphy found Marlon Andrews's passport. When he flipped through the dark blue-covered booklet, he noticed the most recent visa entry was stamped in Denmark nearly eight months before. Like Coulter's passport, there was no exit stamp and no entry stamp into Sweden. Also there was no photo of Andrews. It had been removed.

As Murphy unfolded the sheet of paper, something slid out and dropped back inside the drawer.

Murphy reached in and picked it up. It was a picture. From its miniature size, Murphy guessed it had come from a passport. It was a photo of a young moon-faced man with a harelip and a buzz cut.

When he unfolded the sheet of paper, Murphy discovered it was a DD 214 form for someone by the name of Paul Sullivan. It was a document issued by the United States Veterans Administration following discharge from the U.S. military. It indicated Sullivan had been issued a general discharge from the Marine Corps the previous fall. "This is interesting," Murphy said. "According to this, his last duty station was with the security detail at the U.S. embassy in Copenhagen."

Murphy was pondering the meaning of the two travel documents and the VA form when Romana pointed out something she discovered while standing in the kitchenette.

"John," she said. "Come look in the sink."

Clumps of dark hair and tiny flecks of facial hair dotted the white porcelain. "Someone had a shave and a haircut," Murphy remarked, rubbing a clump of dark hair between his thumb and forefinger. "Quite recently, too. This hair is still damp."

Fifteen minutes had elapsed since Murphy had arrived at the commune. During that time, he had found a body, two American passports, a VA form and evidence someone had cut his hair and shaved not long before he arrived.

Usually, Murphy's instincts told him the meaning of the clues he uncovered, but this time there was no gut reaction.

As they left the cabin and stepped back out into the Swedish sunshine, Murphy shared his quandary to Romana. "I know the man I'm looking for knocked off Mouse, but I've got no idea how all the stuff we found goes together or where he is now."

Murphy had a whole bunch of dots, but no way to connect them. At least not yet.

While standing beside the pond, Murphy lit a cigarette and pondered his next step when he saw the police car, with its lights flashing, turn off the main road and head toward the little steel bridge.

"Uh oh," he said. "It looks like the shit is about to hit the fan."

Murphy flipped his cigarette into the water, grabbed Romana, and quickly stepped back into the cabin.

MURPHY DIDN'T have much time to weave a tale.

There were three people in the cabin. One of them was dead. The other two were alive, and neither of them had a good reason for being there.

This time, Murphy knew he would have to fess up.

"Honesty is always the best policy," Van Dyck advised him once, "Except when you have to lie."

Murphy wasn't averse to stretching the truth, but this was definitely one of those times when a lie would not help him.

Murphy watched through a window in the rear of the cabin as the two policemen walked to the back of the main cottage only to discover that the door was locked.

"They'll be coming this way, soon," Murphy told Romana. He guided her to the cabin's main room. "I'll do the talking. Don't speak unless spoken to."

The most awkward moment came right after the two Swedish policemen walked through the front door of the cabin.

Lund stopped just short of the body, while Gunderson, standing just behind and to one side of the police inspector, drew his pistol.

Murphy put up his hands. "There's no need to do that, pal." He lowered one arm to point at the gun. "I'm a cop, too."

Lund turned his head slightly. In Svenska, he told Gunderson to put his gun down. Then the police inspector quickly switched to English. "I don't understand." He sounded perplexed. "You're an American. What is an American policeman doing here? In Laxa?"

"I'm not a policeman, exactly." Murphy reached across his body with his left arm and tapped the First Cav shoulder patch on his field jacket. "I have my credentials right here."

Lund stared at the shoulder patch. "Credentials?"

Murphy started to take off his field jacket. "May I? My ID card is under the shoulder patch."

Lund nodded. At the same time, he told Gunderson to holster his weapon. Murphy moved to the table where he had found the passports and picked up the scissors. After snipping the stitching from the top of the large shoulder patch, he reached in with his thumb and forefinger and slid his ID card out from its hiding place.

As he offered the little plastic card to Lund, he made a terse introduction. "I'm John Murphy. U.S. Army Criminal Investigation Division." Then he gestured toward Romana. "This is Romana Alley. My friend. She really doesn't know what's going on here."

As he reached for Murphy's ID card, Lund made his introductions. "I'm police inspector Magnus Lund from Mariestad." Then he glanced toward his companion. "My young colleague is officer Ulf Gunderson."

Lund studied the card. He could see the disheveled man standing in front of him bore a passing resemblance to the clean-shaven, well-groomed man in the picture on the ID card.

"And just what is going on here?" the police inspector asked.

Murphy explained. He told Lund about his assignment. He told him what he knew about Marlon Andrews, why he began to tail Mouse in Stockholm, and how he had followed him to Laxa.

Lund looked down at the body. "And how did he die?" he asked.

Murphy leaned over, picked up the dead man's left arm and pointed at the armpit. "One bullet right here," he said. "I think it was a .38. There was no exit wound."

The police inspector nodded. "I've seen this kind of work before."

Lund told Murphy about the man in the canal. "He was killed in the same manner."

Lund looked down at Mouse's body. "How long ago do you think this happened?"

Murphy got down on one knee and leaned over the body. "May I?"

Lund gestured with his right hand. "Be my guest."

Murphy crouched. Then he rolled up one of the dead man's pant legs. Looking up at Lund, he stated: "Judging from the slight amount of lividity—see the reddish tinge on the shin just below the knee—I'd say he died at least two hours ago, no more than three. And that one gunshot killed him instantaneously."

Lund had another question. "And how long have you been here?"

Murphy took no offense to the police inspector's line of inquiry. He would have asked the same question.

Quickly and concisely, Murphy filled in the Swedish police inspector on his travel itinerary.

"We got here about twenty minutes ago," he explained. "We came in on the train from Stockholm. We talked to a boy named Angelo at the Italian restaurant in town. He told us some Americans were living with some hippies out here. We walked out here to check it out."

"Hippies?" Lund commented. "I heard that, too."

Gunderson and Romana stood off to one side as silent witnesses listening as the dialogue between the CID investigator and the Swedish police inspector unfolded.

Murphy stood up. "There's a few things I want to show you." He led Lund to the counter next to the kitchen sink, where he had left the documents he had found. "Maybe, it will help us figure out where Marlon Andrews has gone."

Murphy handed Andrews' passport to Lund. He pointed out the obvious. "Notice the picture has been removed." And the not-so obvious. "Notice his passport was last stamped in Copenhagen. No exit stamp from Denmark. No entry stamp into Sweden."

Lund scanned the passport for a few moments before handing it back to Murphy.

Murphy offered the other passport to Lund. "As you can see, his picture wasn't removed." Then, he glanced down at the body. "That's Mr. Coulter lying on the floor here. His friends called him Mouse."

"I've heard of a man called Mouse," Lund interjected.

The CID investigator pointed at the passport. "You'll notice the passport also was last stamped in Copenhagen when he entered Denmark. Also, no exit stamp and no entry stamp into Sweden."

"Interesting," Lund said. He handed the travel document back to Murphy.

Next, Murphy showed the Swedish police inspector the DD 214. As Lund scrutinized the one-page document, he explained, "This is an extract of Mr. Sullivan's discharge from the U.S. Marine Corps," Then, he pointed to box twelve on the single sheet of paper. "Sullivan's last duty station before his discharge was with the Marine security detachment at the U.S. embassy in Copenhagen."

Finally, Murphy showed Lund the tiny head-and-shoulder shot of Sullivan. "I think Andrews removed this from Sullivan's passport and replaced it with his own picture," he continued. "I think he intends to use Sullivan's passport to get back into the states."

Lund rubbed his chin. "But why Sullivan's passport? Why not use Mr. Coulter's travel papers." He looked down at the body. "He isn't going anywhere."

Murphy had shared Lund's puzzlement. Then, it dawned on him.

"You know, Inspector Lund, maybe, there was something special about Sullivan's passport."

"Special?" the police inspector asked.

Murphy nodded. "Maybe Sullivan was traveling on an official government passport, the kind Uncle Sam issues to people like me. It's got a red cover, and it usually opens doors."

Murphy smiled. "I'd show you mine, but I'm not using it this trip."

"We know." Lund glanced in the direction of the young patrolman. "Officer Gunderson found your passport when he searched your backpack at Reverend Burgess' apartment in Stockholm."

"I thought your names sounded familiar," Murphy commented. "Reverend Fred told me about you."

Interrupting the conversation, Gunderson spoke in Svenska to the police inspector.

Lund nodded. "My young colleague reminded me we saw both of you yesterday sitting on a bench in front of the Swedish Academy in Stockholm," the police inspector said. "Officer Gunderson has quite an eye for detail."

Then Lund got back to business. "Tell me more about this special passport."

"Whenever I've used it, I've never had any trouble clearing customs, no matter what country I was in," Murphy explained. "The last two or three times I've come into Logan—that's the airport in Boston—the customs agents didn't even bother to look through my backpack when I flashed that passport. If Andrews is traveling on one, I don't think anyone will give him a second look."

"You're probably right," Lund agreed.

Murphy wasn't done. "But he would still have problems getting out of Sweden without a hitch if he didn't have an entry stamp, no matter which passport he was carrying," he pointed out.

"Which means Andrews must go to Denmark, the last country Mr. Sullivan legally entered, to travel from Europe," Lund said.

"I agree," Murphy said. "But how?"

"Malmo," Lund replied, "He's going to Malmo."

IT DIDN'T take much to convince Murphy why Malmo, Sweden's third largest city, would be the logical jumping off point for Fish.

It was located about a thirty-minute boat ride across the Oresand Strait from Copenhagen.

"Thousands of people travel each day in both directions," Lund said. "Some live in Denmark and work in Sweden, and some live in Sweden and work in Denmark. There's little passport control. For the most part, they come and go as they please. Our suspect would have no difficulty mingling with these people and slipping back into Denmark aboard one of the ferries."

Murphy noticed how the Swedish police inspector referred to Andrews as "our suspect."

Lund continued, "I believe we should track down this man together. After all, you know what he looks like. You will be able to identify him when we find him."

For Lund, it was a logical step to join forces with Murphy. The police inspector didn't have much more time to work on the case, and the young CID investigator seemed to possess the expertise and the knowledge to be of assistance. Later, they would work out the formalities.

Murphy recalled the photo Smith, the CID agent, showed him in Lubeck. Then, he thought about the hair clippings Romana had discovered in the cabin. There was a good chance Fish still looked like the basic trainee in his military ID photo. Perhaps, he could finger Andrews when they reached Malmo.

The pursuit began with a brief visit to the train station in Laxa.

While Lund conversed with the station master in Svenska, Murphy took Romana aside in a far corner of the small train station.

"Look," he said. "I'm going to go with these guys, no matter where that is, but I don't think you should come with us. I don't want you to get into any trouble, and the more time you spend with the police the more likely that will happen."

Murphy spoke slightly above a whisper. He didn't want Lund to pick up any of what he was saying to Romana. "I hate to leave you here, but I think you would agree it is the best course to follow."

Romana nodded. "I understand, John."

Murphy continued. "We'll put you on the next train to Stockholm."

As Murphy wrapped an arm around Romana's shoulders, he dropped his voice even more. "It was great to see you again, Romana, but things have changed," he whispered. "You've got what you want, and I think I've got what I want."

Romana remained mute. Showing no outward sign of emotion, she simply nodded.

Moments later, Lund walked over to tell Murphy what he had learned.

"The station master informs me the last train through Laxa traveling south to Malmo left about twenty minutes before you arrived from Orebro," the inspector said. "One of the Americans from the commune boarded it."

Murphy frowned. "So Andrews has a ninety-minute head start."

"Yes," Lund nodded. "But he has a long way to go."

The police inspector said the train is going to Gothenburg. "That's about two hundred fifty kilometers to the west," Lund explained. "The train makes several stops along the way, so that leg of the trip will take two-and-a-half hours. After a brief layover in Gothenburg, it will take another four hours for the train to reach Malmo."

Murphy quickly did the math. "So it will take Andrews six-and-a-half to seven hours to reach Malmo," he said. "Can we get there first?"

Lund glanced toward Gunderson, who stood close to the police inspector trying to follow the conversation. "Well, we have officer Gunderson, the best driver in the department, and we have The Rocket," he said, alluding to the brawny American-built police cruiser parked in front of the train station.

Switching to Svenska, Lund spoke to the young patrolman for a few moments.

Murphy looked toward Romana. He wondered whether she was following the conversation between the two Swedes. He hoped she wouldn't offer to translate it for him.

Romana continued to play dumb.

"What are they talking about?" she asked.

Murphy shrugged. "Search me."

Abruptly, Lund reverted to English. "Officer Gunderson informs me it is about five hundred kilometers from here to Malmo, and he assures me we can make the trip in a little more than three hours if we hurry."

Then, the police inspector turned to Romana.

"I don't think you should accompany us to Malmo, miss," Lund said. "The trip is potentially dangerous, and, if something were to happen to you, I would have a lot of explaining to do." Then, he pointed toward Murphy. "If something were to happen to your friend Mr. Murphy, then he would have a lot of explaining to do."

If Romana was surprised to hear about the police inspector's plans for her, she didn't let on. "I understand, Inspector," is all she said.

Murphy also didn't reveal his reaction to Lund's intentions. It caught him by surprise, but he was relieved he didn't have to bring the subject up.

"I've arranged for a seat for you on the next train to Stock-holm, Miss Alley," Lund said. He looked down at his watch. "It leaves in about a half hour, so you should be back home around eleven thirty."

"If it doesn't cloud up, you may still see some sun when you get home," the police inspector added. "Hopefully, Mr. Murphy and I will have our suspect in custody by then."

"SO, MR. MURPHY, how did you meet Miss Alley?" Lund asked.

The question came about thirty minutes into the trip to Malmo.

At soon as the Dodge Polara began barreling south down Highway 50 with its lights flashing and Gunderson at the steering wheel, the police inspector began fiddling with the dials on the police radio.

At one point, he apologized to Murphy. "The national police board is trying to improve the police communication system here in Sweden," he said. "At the moment, it is a nightmare."

It didn't help that Lund seldom used the radio. It took awhile for him to raise the police station in Laxa. He reported the location of Mouse's body and the circumstances surrounding his death.

Next, the police inspector had the dispatcher in Laxa patch him through to his headquarters in Mariestad. "Officer Gunderson and I are traveling south in pursuit of a murderer," he reported. "We're following up a lead. No need for further assistance at this time."

Pointedly, the police inspector didn't reveal how far south he intended to travel.

Then, Lund reminded the young patrolman piloting The Rocket to limit the use of the klaxon while the Dodge sped south at about 150 kilometers per hour. "Just use the flashers, Ulf," he said. "Don't use the klaxon unless absolutely necessary."

Finally, the police inspector, who sat in the front passenger seat, turned his attention to Murphy, who had been sitting in the back watching the forest of trees whiz past. While unable to follow anything that Lund was saying on the radio, he had listened to the Swedish dialogue intently nonetheless.

"Excuse me, what did you say?" Lund's switch to English caught Murphy off guard.

"I asked how you and Miss Alley met."

Murphy told Lund about his assignment at Kagnew Station three summers before.

"I was working undercover there, too, and we just happened to meet," he said. "She helped me out, and we became friends."

Murphy didn't share any details about the case, and Lund didn't probe, but the Swedish police inspector wanted to know more about Romana and what she was doing in Sweden.

"She's a nurse," Murphy said. "She's part of a humanitarian mission to obtain medical supplies for hospitals in Eritrea."

Murphy went on to tell Lund Sweden had a history of providing such aid to the Ethiopian province. He didn't tell the police inspector about Zula and Senait nor reveal Romana's efforts to train them for the Eritrean rebels' medical corps.

Lund, apparently satisfied with Murphy's answers to his questions, probed no further.

Van Dyck would have been proud, Murphy thought. "There's a big difference between an error of omission and an error of commission," the old warrant officer told him. "It's not a lie if you don't tell it."

Gunderson gunned the Dodge through the woods down Highway 50 for about an hour before hooking up with the E4 near Odesburg.

This portion of the highway ran along the eastern shore of Lake Vattern. When Murphy made the trip up the E4 to Stockholm on the night he arrived in Sweden the lake had been shrouded in darkness. Reverend Fred had rolled past it at a much more leisurely pace, but Murphy still had been unaware such a large body of water was located there.

The conversation between Lund and Murphy resumed.

"How long have you been in the army, Mr. Murphy?" the police inspector asked.

"Nearly twelve years."

"Have you ever been posted to Vietnam?" Lund continued.

"I did two one-year tours and a part of a third." Murphy paused, just for one beat. "I got a little shot up and came home early, but I'm all right now."

Lund didn't pry. Murphy didn't tell him about the tiny bits of shrapnel that occasionally worked their way out through his skin.

"Personally, I have no opinion about your country's involvement in Vietnam," Lund said. "In Sweden, people are allowed to stand on the middle ground, neither for nor against."

Murphy chuckled. "In America, there is no middle ground. You have to be either for or against something. Those are the only two choices."

Apparently, Lund understood American political culture.

"Don't get me wrong, there are people in Sweden who strongly support what the United States is doing in Vietnam," Lund went on. "You were in Stockholm yesterday near the peace demonstration. As you can see, there also are people in Sweden who are vehemently opposed to it."

The police inspector paused for a moment to say a few words in Svenska to Gunderson, who never took his eyes off the road but smiled as he responded with a few words.

Lund translated. "It sounds like Officer Gunderson would gladly go to Vietnam to help you," the police inspector said, with the hint of a grin on his face. "'Kill a Commie for Christ,' is what he said."

Murphy had heard that before. Van Dyck had used the same term to describe the depth of loathing the South Korean troops fighting in South Vietnam had for their Communist adversary.

Murphy chuckled. "A friend of mine used to say that."

Then he got serious.

"Look, I really don't know how I feel about the war, but I do know I don't like the idea of your country allowing deserters from our military to live here," Murphy confided.

"I understand," Lund said. He sounded truly conciliatory. "But I really think our willingness to open our doors to them has more to do with economics and less to do with politics. Frankly, Sweden has a labor shortage, and we need people to come here to work. As long as they become good Swedes, we really don't care who they are."

Murphy understood what Lund was doing. He often did the same when he was working with someone he hadn't met before. You needed to see what made them tick to know whether you could work well together.

Apparently, Murphy had passed the test.

"I can see you're a man with convictions, Mr. Murphy, but, like all of us, sometimes you have your doubts," Lund observed. "I know I have mine. We should get along fine."

Murphy agreed. "It's always good to know who you're working with." He had no problems with the serious but easy-going Swedish police inspector.

Gunderson didn't switch on the klaxon until he had to negotiate his way past a long line of cars near a traffic accident on the stretch of the highway that snaked through the industrial city of Jonkoping. Once they cleared the scene, the young patrolman resumed cruising speed and cut off the sound.

About a half-hour later, near Ljungby, Gunderson had to resort to using the klaxon again. This time, it was to warn the elderly driver of a car headed north on the wrong side of the road. The old man, who was driving at an extremely slow rate of speed, pulled off onto the shoulder to give way as the fast-moving police car sped south.

After stealing a glance in the rearview mirror, Gunderson said a few words in Svenska.

"It's been almost four years since we began driving on the right side of the road," Lund explained to Murphy. "Some of the old-timers forget that sometimes and have to be reminded." Then, the police inspector issued a rare grin. "Officer Gunderson said we just scared the shit—I think that's the proper word—out of that old man."

"That's exactly the right word," Murphy agreed.

The final leg of the trip passed by in silence.

As Gunderson predicted, they arrived in Malmo well ahead of the train from Gothenburg.

The young policeman drove them to the central train station, located directly across a canal from the Hotel Savoy, where the opening scene of the detective novel Lund had started reading two days before took place.

Even at this late in the day, the train station was bustling.

It didn't take Lund long to decide the crowded platform was not the best place to confront Marlon Andrews.

"He could be armed, and he's already killed at least three times," Lund said, explaining the dilemma to Murphy. "There are only three of us and if we try to take him here, some bystander may get hurt."

Surveying the scene, Murphy reluctantly agreed.

"But where do we try to take him then?" It was a good question. Lund spent a few moments of conversation in Svenska with Gunderson, and the young patrolman supplied the answer.

"Officer Gunderson has frequently traveled through Malmo to play hockey in Denmark." Lund announced, switching to English. "He said the best place to make the pinch, as he called it, was down at the ferry slip."

Lund continued. "It's large open area, Officer Gunderson tells me, and there shouldn't be that many people around there this time night."

IT TOOK JUST a few minutes after leaving the train station for Murphy and Lund to agree on a plan of action at the ferry slip.

First, Gunderson parked the police cruiser on a side street out of sight of the dock and in the opposite direction from the train station.

Next, the young policeman was stationed on the quay near the water's edge. Gunderson patrolled the area between two docked ferryboats. He slowly walked back and forth, occasionally tipping his cap to the prettier female passengers. He didn't look out of place.

Murphy and Lund stood together away from the edge of the pier no more than ten meters from the patrolman. The two men appeared to be thoroughly engrossed in deep conversation, but Murphy's head was on a swivel. He kept an eye on the people approaching the broad quay from the direction of the train station.

They waited.

It was late, but night hadn't fallen yet. The last vestiges of the sun appeared in purples, reds and pinks on the western horizon as it slowly descended. Even in the gloaming, Murphy could make out the features of the few stragglers, mostly young couples, walking to catch a ride to Copenhagen.

The two Swedish policemen and the CID investigator had to play their roles for no more than thirty minutes before Andrews appeared.

Fish was easy to pick out. He looked exactly like the picture Smith had shown Murphy three days earlier in Lubeck, right down to his boot-camp buzz cut.

As Andrews slowly walked across the quay, the crew aboard

195

one of the ferries prepared to cast off. Fish picked up the pace and started to run toward the boat. Except for Murphy and Lund, nobody stood between him and the ferry.

Murphy called out as Andrews ran past him. He told him to stop. Apparently, Fish didn't hear him. As the ferry began to slowly pull away from the dock, he ran faster in his effort to catch up with it.

Gunderson's attention now was drawn to the man dashing across the quay toward the ferry. He looked back toward Lund, who appeared to be reaching inside his jacket for the pistol in his shoulder holster. Following the police inspector's lead, the young patrolman, who was standing much closer to the boat, quickly drew his pistol.

"*Stanna! Annars Shjuter jag!*" Gunderson yelled, taking careful aim with his pistol.

Immediately, Lund shouted out the English translation, "Stop! Or I'll shoot."

Too late.

As Andrews leapt from the dock to the ferry, Gunderson fired twice.

Andrews didn't miss the ferry by much. His torso slammed into the hard rubber bumper on the little boat's stern and then pin-wheeled back into the water in the boat's wake. The backwash from the ferry rammed Andrews into the stone quay.

Murphy and Gunderson got down on their knees and leaned over the side of the dock. It was a struggle, but they were able to pull Andrews out of the water and carry him a few feet onto the pier.

Murphy could see where one of Gunderson's rounds had hit Andrews in the back of his right shoulder. When he rolled him onto his back on the stone dock he found no exit wound.

Andrews was unconscious. His body lay inert. No movement.

No twitching. No moaning.

"This guy's in trouble," Murphy told Lund. "I think he went into cardiac arrest."

Murphy, who once trained as a medic during an undercover assignment at Fort Sam Houston in San Antonio, got on his knees next to Andrews. Following his training, he began to administer cardiac pulmonary resuscitation.

First, he tried mouth-to-mouth respiration for about forty seconds. Then, as he learned in his training, he tried chest compression with his palms of both hands for about the same amount of time.

Nothing. No response.

Murphy looked up to Lund, who was hovering over him. "I think he's gone."

Before he spoke again, the CID investigator turned to watch the ferry boat grow smaller as it exited the Suelshammen, Malmo's inner harbor.

"I don't think the bullet killed him." Murphy said. "He must have broken his neck when he slammed into the back of the boat or when he hit the pier. There wasn't much blood from the bullet wound. I think he was dead when we took him out of the water."

Murphy reached across the body and rolled up the sleeve of Andrews' jacket. He showed Lund the scar on the dead man's right wrist.

The police inspector was curious. "Shrapnel? In Vietnam?"

Murphy shook his head. "No. Box cutter. Safeway."

Lund didn't understand. "Safeway? What is Safeway?"

"It's a chain of supermarkets," Murphy explained. "He worked in a Safeway before he joined the Army."

From his pocket, Murphy pulled out the crumpled white business card Smith had given him in Lubeck. He looked at the handwritten telephone number. For a moment, Murphy thought about the call he would make and what he would say. Then, he slipped the card back into his pocket.

"So, I can take one of these ferries to Copenhagen?" he asked.

"*Ja,*" the police inspector answered. He looked at his watch. "This time of night, a boat leaves Malmo every thirty minutes or so. Last boat is at midnight."

Lund looked down at the body.

"What do we do with him?" the police inspector asked.

"He's all yours," Murphy said. "I don't handle trash." Then he stood up. "I just want to go home."

"Ja," Lund agreed. "I do, too."

Buy Paul Betit's books

❏ *Phu Bai*

It is June 1967, and United States military involvement in South Vietnam is nearing its zenith. As the war ratchets up, John Murphy and Charles Van Dyck of the Army's Criminal Investigation Division investigate the murder of an American soldier at Phu Bai. War intrudes as the two investigators build their case against the most likely suspect. But a bizarre twist turns it into an unusual manhunt in the middle of a war zone.

Softcover, pages 224, JWB Edition 2006. Price: $17.95

❏ *Kagnew Station*

In this sequel to Phu Bai, CID investigator John Murphy travels to a remote U.S. military base in East Africa during the summer of 1968 to investigate the mysterious death of an American soldier. Evidence points to a marauding band of Eritrean rebels. The investigation becomes personal when someone tries to kill Murphy, still coming to grips with his Vietnam War experience. Murphy uncovers the identity of the murderer but faces an unusual dilemma while wrapping up the case.

Softcover, pages 256, 2005. Price: $17.95 US

❏ *The Man in the Canal*

In the summer of 1971, Army CID investigator John Murphy goes undercover to find a murderer hiding among the U.S. military deserters who have taken refuge in Sweden during the Vietnam War. At the same time, Swedish police inspector Magnus Lund tries to learn the identity of a dead man found floating in the historic Göta Canal. The two investigators work independently until a thread of clues bring them together for an exciting climax.

Softcover, pages 208, 2014. Price: 18.95 US

Buy the books above at amazon.com, bn.com or jstwrite.com, order them through your local bookstore or use the order form below.

Send payment made payable to:

Paul Betit, PO Box 384, Brunswick, ME 04011

Please send me the books I have checked above. I'm enclosing $_____
(please add $3.00 for the first book and $1.00 for each additional book to cover postage.) Send a check or money order—no cash or C.O.D.s. Prices and shipping fees are subject to change without notice.

Name _____

Address _____

City _____ State _____ Zip Code _____
(Allow 2 weeks for delivery) This offer is subject to withdrawal without notice.

Autographed copies are available through paulbetit.com

CPSIA information can be obtained at www.ICGtesting.com
Printed in the USA
BVOW02s1735070114

341105BV00005B/14/P

9 781934 949856